MAYSUN AND THE WINGFISH

Alison Lock

Also by Alison Lock

A Slither of Air (Indigo Dreams Publishing 2011)
Above the Parapet (Indigo Dreams Publishing 2013)
Beyond Wings (Indigo Dreams Publishing 2015)

MAYSUN AND THE WINGFISH

Alison Lock

MM

Mother's Milk Books

For my boys

1

Flicking their lithe rudders they spit beads of water onto Maysun's face. She laughs and splutters before diving again.

'Wingfish are so beautiful!' she says to Pa, afterwards. Pa frowns. Maysun is on the bank pulling her shawl around her while her hair drips onto her shoulders. She notices the tiny button scales that have caught on her skin, and she smiles.

'Kiri quar kiri!' calls Maysun, singing out the words. The fish respond by twisting up in a playful fountain. The Wingfish are speckled in a rainbow of colours. Such beauty is unusual in the world of Watterishi, a place where grey skies and green-brown land merge into a camouflage.

Pa lets out a loud bellow. The fish turn, shift as one and head toward the centre of the lake, diving down, staying there until the surface is still. The Wingfish are an enigma to him, but he believes they will understand him by the tone of his voice.

'That's it for today,' he says.

'Shouldn't we throw some back for the Wingfish?' Maysun asks, glancing at the nets full of the Gringrow garlands.

'Huh,' Pa scoffs. 'There's barely enough for us.'

'But Omma says we must be kind.'

'You still have much to learn, my girl. The Wingfish will survive long after we are gone.'

Maysun looks up. The clouds are hanging in vertical streams, tinged yellow. Behind them she can see the moon, looming, its outline tattered by the cloud.

'The moon is almost full,' she says. 'Although...' her voices shakes, as she thinks of her mother's warnings, 'one side is brighter.'

'Don't worry,' Pa reassures her. 'Everything is fine.' He gazes up at the fulgid clouds. His daughter is right. Even he, who doesn't care for the fears of the women and the elders, can see that there is something peculiar about the sky.

It has been three score years since Ares came within a whisker of the planet, sending shudders through to the core. No one knows why it happens, when it will happen, why it appears to chase the full moon, or why the moon changes colour becoming red and looming large. But when Ares comes close every creature cowers in fear of its destructive force. The older Watterishi are fearful of the full moon and bide their time until it has passed. The elders no longer speak of the planet they fear as if by doing so might invoke an evil omen. To minify the bad forces, the Elders rarely eat the Wingfish, although at times they are driven by hunger to sacrifice a few. But by way of compensation, they give back one tenth of the Gringrows they collect, always leaving enough for the Wingfish. They believe that as long as the Wingfish are happy, the moon chaser will never strike.

Pa and Maysun collect their bundles of coiled vegetation and set off towards the village. Maysun looks forward to seeing Omma as she knows she will be pleased with their day's gatherings. Maysun will not mention the lake they have left behind, or that it is almost stripped bare. She thinks about the cooked Gringrow plaits they will eat later that night. She wishes they could gather the balls of fungus that grow under the earth at the edge of the forest. They are so succulent when fresh. But it is early in the season and Gringrows must do tonight with a few of the dried mushrooms that remain from the last season. Maysun's mouth waters as they walk along the muddy path. Their sacks are heavy, and she stops for a moment's rest. She looks towards the west at another empty lake where the vegetation has been almost all stripped and there is little to hold the bank in place, leaving the waters to swirl and thicken with mud or break over the edge of the thin soil. Rain begins to fall.

Even the lake they have left behind is starting to drain away. This season the Watterishi have gone too far; they have plucked at the roots of the Gringrow that once held firm the sides of the lakes. Maysun can hear oozing and bubbling as the Wingfish writhe in the shallows. They are agitated. Their gills click, and the surface begins to lather. The Wingfish are gathering and following one another, head to tail. They circle around and around and in the centre is the largest of their kind. The giant Wingfish is sweeping his fins around him like a grand cape, his dorsal fin stands erect and proud. One blow of his tail and the sting would be fatal. The others continue their circling, and they swim according to their instinct, drifting on their backs, stirring up the water with their floatier fins spreading out around them. They nibble on each other's tails, and when the primo Wingfish shoots upwards out of the lake, they are too busy to notice his twisting loops and triple flips.

If the villagers were to stand on their roofs, they would see the glitter of scales flashing in the pall of the moon. The village consists of huts, lifted up from the ground by stilts; the ground beneath them is often flooded. Each dwelling is made from the strong branches of the Ruba to form the uprights, which are waxy and waterproof and will not rot in the waters. Between many of the huts run laddered bridges, woven from the reeds. The smaller Ruba leaves are used as roof tiles. The reeds grow alongside the rivers in the smooth running waters where the Gringrows do not thrive. These reeds form the woven sides of the huts and the fencing around the verandas that protrude from their sides. From these, the inhabitants can see out across their valley, they can look into the dark Ruba forests and they can see the bright moon as it appears above the mountain peaks. In the gloom of the evenings, they sit on their verandas calling out across the valleys in ululations and glottal clicks, their Ruba-bean oil candles glinting from within their huts.

Omma recognises the footsteps of her daughter and husband on the path and as they climb the ladder their steps are echoed by a distant thump, not unlike the rolling thunder that signals the beginning of a storm.

In fact, the sound is made by the primo male back at the Gringrow lake, as he lands hard on the shore.

Slap, slap, slap.

The vibrations ripple across the lake and the muddy shores, girding the others into action. The air is heavy with rain and thick clouds. Within each cloud are ripe puffballs filled with watery spores, expanding and bursting. There is so much water in the atmosphere that the fish can swim for short bursts in the air high above the surface of the lake.

'Loa,' Omma says, greeting her husband and daughter. 'What would I do without my gatherers?' Omma asks as father and daughter climb over the top step of the ladder and into the hut. Omma takes the burden of the sacks. They rub noses.

'So, how were the Wingfish today?' Omma casts a nervous look at her husband. 'I've heard that the moon is on the fast rise.'

'Just gossip,' he replies.

Pa is already relaxing in his rocking chair. He has that do not disturb look. He has taken the eyeglass from the drawer, the one that is Omma's and that once belonged to her mother. It has many colours: green, orange, yellow, blue, but rarely the violet puce of warning. Pa likes the eyeglass. It calms him, it gives him sweet dreams, assures him that the world will carry on as always.

Pa does not carry the terrible anxieties that seeped into the lives of the Watterishi over the generations — the constant fear of attack from that place of ice beyond the Ruba trees. Since the day he broke through the amniotic sac to his father's delight and the weary awe of his mother, there has only been one interruption: they called it the Soomoon to end all Soomoons. It came after the rise of the last Red Moon, rocking the planet, leaving many dead. Pa was just a baby. He and his family survived, but rarely spoke of the trauma.

The Watterishi continued to fear the Peakerfolk. But it had been an unlikely blessing that when the planet of Ares chased the full moon around their world, shaking and rumbling the planet with a full Soomoon, that it had caused the rapid rise of the Ruba trees. Some claimed that the Soomoon had drawn out great mineral deposits from below the surface of the planet and that it was the scattering of these small rocks on the slopes of the mountainside that had encouraged the proliferation of the Ruba trees. Others dismissed this theory. In any case, the result had been clear — there was now an absolute division of the world of the Watterishi from the mountain tribes of the Peakerfolk. From that time on the fights and battles had subsided.

The less fortunate effect of the Soomoon was that many, but not all of the copper mines had closed up, leaving the Watterishi without access to a good supply of metal. Now they must recycle the remnants of the implements they made before the Soomoon.

For the Watterishi, there is nowhere else to go: their

land, their world, this valley is all they have. They believe that its steep sides end at the mountain tops falling into nothingness beyond. And the rivers that race towards the waterfalls slip over the edge into never-ending cloud. Therefore, the Watterishi have no desire to venture beyond the borders of their lands, no inclination to risk falling into the abyss.

Pa sees a shifting light within the eyeglass: bolts of silver arrows are shooting from right to left, east to west. He watches with interest at first, eye wide with curiosity. The silver bolts quiver and float before his eyes, then they waver and fall, and then he is watching a dull brown cloud that turns orange, reddening the longer he watches. He takes out the eyeglass, blinks, rubs both eyes, circles his eyeballs and replaces the glass back into the socket of his other eye. The silver arrows are still there, but now they are coming towards him, crackling in the swiftness of their flight. He cannot look at them as he fears they will pierce his eye. He shakes his head, takes out the eyeglass, tuts and tuts again.

'What is it?' Omma asks.

Pa cannot make sense of what he has seen, but he knows it must have some meaning, a message, a sign. Pa stands up abruptly, leaving the rocking chair still in motion. He puts the eyeglass into the drawer, his back still to Omma. The creaking rhythm of the chair continues.

'What is it?' Omma asks, she is more concerned now, her turquoise eyes widening. 'Is that eyeglass giving you bad dreamings?'

Pa is shaking his head.

'You know it means nothing. You've said yourself that it is all superstition from the old times when the ancestors believed that the glass foretold the future.'

Pa still does not respond, neither does he turn around.

He is staring at the crystal bowl that holds the Deathfish. The Watterishi believe that a house that contains a Deathfish keeps the mortal ones safe. The great geode bowl had been created by Pa's father, chipped and chiselled until the molten edges were made smooth, leaving the sides frosted, semi-opaque. These days they are usually green, darkened with slime, the Deathfish occluded, but today as Pa gazes at his reflection, the Deathfish appears. Pa's face is superimposed into the gape of the mouth with the sharp white fangs. Pa's face crumples, and, for a moment, he sees only a monster, a parody of a dorsalled man.

'I hope you left plenty of Gringrows for the fish,' Omma is saying, pulling at the stash of curly greens.

Meanwhile, the Wingfish are stirring. The clicks become a drone increasing in volume. Any Gringrow that Maysun and Pa did not collect has been eaten; the lake is scoured of every last frond. The hungry fish swirl around, diving into the undergrowth but soon they return, collapsing in the shallow waters. Even the primo male slumps back to the shore, but underneath his glistening scales is a burning glow, fired with anguish that increases with his fury.

Omma has the copper pan ready, heating up the water over the flames of the oil-burner. The Gringrows are next to her, ready for the pot, laid out in neat plaits. Maysun is watching as Omma picks up each plait and places it into the bubbling liquid. She also notices the new coil on Omma's head, how her dark hair is interwoven with reed shafts and shaped like an upturned bowl. She will easily be able to carry the beans of the Ruba when they are picked. Maysun touches her own head and wonders when it will be time for her to have a hair bowl. Omma's skin is shining in the low light.

'Have there been visitors today?' Pa asks, touching Omma's shoulder, letting his hand slide down the length of her smooth arm.

'Only Raisa the Elder,' Ma replies.

'Ah, that mongerer of fear,' Pa says.

'She was wanting to teach us younger women the art of the catch-basket,' Omma says.

'I see,' Pa says, slowly, and lifts an eyebrow towards Maysun.

Omma nods.

'Come on, drink up,' Omma says, briskly. She holds out a cup to Maysun. It is full to the brim of white liquid. It has been drained from the bark, boiled, and its evaporations collected in the cup-like nodes of the Ruba stems. 'It will make you grow into a strong woman.'

Maysun pulls a face and holds her nose as the liquid is tipped into her mouth. Pa puts his hands on his hips.

'Ruba is good for many things,' Pa advises. He has a stern expression. 'In the old days, we feared the Wingfish but now we have learned to live in harmony with them, although...'

'The Wingfish mean no harm,' Maysun says, her lips quivering.

Pa rubs his chin and frowns before continuing. 'You cannot be sure,' he says. 'We have to protect our own.'

'I remember my grandmother making a catch basket,' Omma says. 'The Ruba stalks were sharpened and pushed into the ends of the baskets, like arrowheads pointing inwards...' then as if to demonstrate, she places one hand under the opposite arm. 'If the Wingfish tried to escape...' she clamps the arm to her side with a slap, trapping her hand. Ma's voice trails off, she looks upset, distracted, and turns away from Maysun and Pa.

Pa leans towards Maysun and lowers his voice. 'The

danger time has a name. I will tell you, but you must never speak the word.'

Maysun's eyes widen. She is at once fearful but proud that Pa is willing to confide in her. She knows only too well the importance of spoken words. The Watterishi are discreet with their speech, never careless. Even the women who meet to weave the Ruba fibres, or grind the Ruba beans, or felt the cloth, converse mainly in wordless song. But none of that means that they care any the less for their fellow Watterishi. On the contrary, it is because of their respect for the community that they take such care of their words.

Pa leans forward and whispers into her ear. 'Soomoon,' he croons. 'Soomoon.'

Omma has heard nothing, and Pa looks guilty as she returns with a shawl to wrap around her daughter. It is made from the down of the reed-mace and is soft and comforting against her skin. 'Don't worry, we never have to make the basket traps now,' she says.

Maysun wonders at her father and his way with words. He taught her the tongue of the Peakerfolk, which he learned from his father, and now he has given her this special, secret word.

The approaching rain clouds are sweeping over the mountains. They linger at their apex before dropping their load in the far valley. The watercourses are filled until the mud banks begin to break and slip away. The swirling waters form whirlpools that snap the delicate new buds of the Gringrow from their roots. The fish are dragged along with the flow.

That night, the Watterishi are laid out on their Ruba mats in their huts, their bellies full, their eyes tightly shut, their chests rising and falling in a regular rhythm with the beating of the rain. Dried Gringrow leaves rustle from the rafters, lulling the dwellers to sleep, as silently, the waters rise. Up the stilts, slowly at first, and then rising over the nodes and forks at the points where the stilts have been strengthened.

Maysun leans out to watch the rippling reflection of the silvery moon dispersed and sent shimmering by the falling raindrops. 'Soomoon, Soomoon,' she whispers. 'Soomoon.'

Omma and Pa hear nothing even though they are not sleeping. As the moonlight steals through the reedy walls of their abode, it catches the oily glisten of their skins as they entwine and perform their love-making. By dawn, their gleaming bodies are as slippery as the fish in the lake.

2

Maysun awakes to the lap of water slapping at the underside of the dwelling. The rain has eased but still it slips gently from the sky.

'It'll soon abate,' Pa is saying, looking out across the valley.

Maysun shivers as she watches the moving water that seems to be hurtling down the valleys towards the end of the world. She looks across at the midden on the far bank. The pile of detritus that has always been out of reach of the river is being drawn into it, slowly, piece by piece. Apart from the movement of the water, everything else is strangely still: there is no wind, the trees are motionless, the air is quiet, suspended. The valley and all in it are captured within a vacuum as if breathlessly waiting to be released from their wet embrace. The waters of the valley have swollen like this before, but Maysun has a sense that this time it is different, that something has changed. It is as if the air is pressing against her, there is a sense of waiting, a closing in. She remembers saying the forbidden word in the dark of the night, how it so easily and delightfully slipped from her lips. Surely a word cannot have such power.

The Watterishi go about their daily chores, at first, within the confines of their huts while the waters are still swirling. Later in the day when the waters have calmed they glide about on their reed boats, bartering and exchanging their goods. It is as if nothing has changed. Until one woman slips as she climbs from the raft onto the ladder at the base of a hut with a sack filled with Gringrows. Before anyone can catch hold of her, she is surrounded by angry Wingfish, who nudge and yank and draw her under the surface. She is gone, and the water has quickly folded over the place where she was seen. The woman's daughter is pointing and yelling out to the others, her young son is wailing. Some of the Watterishi have taken to their boats and they are shouting and using their sticks to hit the surrounding water, trying to frighten off the Wingfish. One man is lowered from a hut on a knotted rope but before he reaches the surface the Wingfish snap and bite his feet and legs until the blood flows and he daren't go on.

While all this is going on, and before anyone can stop her, Maysun dives in, slipping seamlessly between the whirlpools. Omma screams, but it is too late. Below the surface of the water Maysun can see very little through the murk and mud. The Wingfish nudge at her ankles, but they do not attack her. Some of the Wingfish are still gnawing at the sack of Gringrows on the woman's back as Maysun disentangles her, leaving the Wingfish to devour the contents. She hauls the woman back up to the surface and they are both pulled up onto the ladder. The woman is carried to the nearest hut and tilted onto her side, letting the water issue from her mouth until she emits a sound that indicates she is alive. The Watterishi might be safe for now, but the Wingfish are hungry.

Maysun shivers as she dries herself. She stares down at the water; she cannot feel brave, or heroic, only guilty. She knows that the word she whispered into the night has opened a chasm. She believes she has cast a spell that will change the world. Her words have given tongue to an old curse, and it is out there, flitting through the reeds, circling the stilt legs of the dwellings, rising into the clammy air.

Silently, the women gather on the balconies. They look down at the water and throw in tiny parcels of Gringrows gathered together with sinews of Ruba. But even as they watch, with an unexpected vigour, the Wingfish snatch at their gifts leaping out of the water towards their hands. An arm is grazed by the abrasive scales and drops of blood spill. The Wingfish become more agitated, twisting and snapping at the hands of the Watterishi who know for certain that they can no longer trust them. Raisa is standing alone at the corner of her hut. She lets out a great ululation that lifts into the air; it rises, rebounding from hut to hut, encircling the entire village. They must begin the work of their ancestors: the making of the catch baskets.

The women all turn towards the sound, their eyes round with fear, while the Wingfish dive below the water's surface. The women know what they must do. Without speaking they make their way across the woven bridges towards Raisa's dwelling. They bring together everything they need: the leaves, fibres, stems and bowls of the sticky solution that they have boiled and squeezed from the scraps of the Ruba. But it is only Raisa who holds the patterns for making the catch baskets and there has not been time to share the knowledge. First, they pile everything into the centre of a circle, and they sit cross-legged, pulling at the tangled bundles, drawing out the lengths to begin to weave the sharp edged catch baskets. Soon the stripped bark has sliced into their unskilled hands, and they are sucking at their cuts as the blood runs through their fingers.

The men are leaning over the corners of the balconies. They smoke their pipes, blinking away the drops of rain and spitting into the draining waters. All the streams and brooks from the hills have joined together forming a fast-moving river that spins around the legs of the dwellings. Branches and rushes and mud are pulled from the banks, gathering and swirling around and around. The Watterishi shiver with the strangeness of the rising waters.

The men spit faster, the fish click and click, and the women weave their traps.

Dusk comes, and the hungry Wingfish have found their natural groupings. The clicking is louder now; pectoral fins flap against hollow bodies. Inside each of the females are eggs ready to be laid, but the vital energies of the primo Wingfish are not focussed on new life, they are surging in fury at the Gringrow stealers. As the Wingfish brush against one another they begin to glow as bright as the moon that is flooding the land with an eerie rose tint. The moon is low, hardly risen above the cusp of the planet, it is reddened, almost as red as the fluid drawn by the sword-edged leaves of the Ruba, as red as the blood on the women's hands. There is a sudden shift, a crackle in the atmosphere, and then a violent movement that causes a frisson of fear to run through the Watterishi.

A blanket of darkness has descended, dropping like the fall of heavy ropes, a blindness from above. All their senses feel smothered, all are holding their breath, wide-eyed, but unable to see.

The Watterishi hear the sound of snapping in the air. The clicking has become a clattering and a hissing. The women stand up, their baskets incomplete, their trapdoors unfinished, their fibres hanging loosely, but now they must try to save themselves. They send their children into the huts where they hunker in the corners, covering their ears. The men and the women on the balconies are waiting.

'The moon has turned,' Raisa says, urging the women to finish their work. 'The Wingfish are rising, ready to attack.'

They watch, transfixed, by the rise of a towering

cyclone of Wingfish. But the red orb of the moon is becoming larger, and then they see it is followed by another, not a moon, but a planet; a planet that is grey. They fear that this planet will push the moon towards them, but the moon glows red and remains before them.

There is a flash from above. The ground below is rumbling, the waters quiver. Bolts of firelight cross and re-cross before the eyes of the Watterishi. Shards of lightning flare, pluming out across the valley. A terrible noise fills the air as the darkness in all its shades of grey and black and red explodes.

There is nothing they can do but crouch in their huts and pray that the waters do not sweep them away over the precipitous edge into the abyss. They pray that the clamouring Wingfish do not rise up to steal them. They pray that their children will be saved. Some are weeping, some are angry. Those that have remained on the balconies are shouting at the sky, thrusting their catch baskets at the moon as if to show it that they will defend themselves. Then they see that the angered Wingfish have risen. They are rising above the level of the platforms, dotting the air as their bodies catch the red light. They can be heard flitting and buzzing, louder and louder, until the noise is overwhelming and no one can hear the screams and the shouts of the other Watterishi. The air is filled with the jostling bodies and fins of the raging Wingfish.

There is a temporary lull from the snapping Wingfish when, momentarily, they dive down into the muddy waters that swirl around the dwelling posts. The Watterishi remain, still, hiding in their huts. But now the Wingfish are rising again, and this time they rise higher. Before long they are flaying the Ruba roof tiles with their teeth, pulling at the mats, snatching at the coils of hair on the women's heads. All screams are lost. The creaking sides of the huts shake as they are torn apart by the Wingfish. Some try to escape and jump into the seething waters, others cover themselves with blankets and leaves and anything they can find to hide themselves.

Those who have remained outside, braving the wrath of the Wingfish, throw Ruba ropes towards each other. They hope that they can stem the destruction by circling the girth of the huts and joining them to each other. Finally, they have used the last rope, and still, the creaking huts that are held together begin to break apart, piece by piece. Some of the dwellings are disappearing, sinking into the waters, others are stripped, flayed of their fibres. Everything is being pulled apart by the Wingfish: the plaited ties, dried stems, sap glue, every leaf of Ruba, all flying away in the wind or sinking into the ever-rising muddy waters.

The red moon is close, it seems to be almost touching. With it comes a great wind. The Watterishi are clinging to the poles with the water rushing around them, the Wingfish catch at them with their quill-like tails, their mouths biting. Many of the Watterishi can no longer hold on and are swept away into the surging waters. Some are submerged for a short time but rise again. Some are drawn into the muddy swamps where they come face to face with the grotesque creatures that lurk in the silt. Disturbed now, the carrion feeders have risen to the surface for the first time, stretching wide their throats and yowling their displeasure at the heavens. The surviving Watterishi are left clinging to pieces of driftwood, clumps of tiles, the remains of the rafts until they are dragged further and further from their homes with each rising wave.

3

From the mountain tops the night-storms had pierced the skyline with bolts of lightning, searing into singular points and gathering and rumbling in a series of crescendoes. To the Peakerfolk it was as if the old gods had risen and were cursing the peaks, hissing and bellowing at all who lived on the mountain. The red light of the moon had cast a strange glow over the crags, colouring the snow-covered ground with a blood-like tinge. As the planet of Ares had come closer to the Red Moon, a wind raged through the crevasses, the rocks of the mountains had growled, the earth beneath them had shaken, and the highest peaks of the Mountains of Qar had split. From the Peakerfolk lands, huge rocks could be seen rolling down the mountain sides to the east, although few remained outside to witness the terrors of the storm.

But now, in the stillness of dawn all is quiet, subdued by the unsparing rush of the storm that has left its traces in open fault-lines and narrow zigzags through the shaken ground. The ice is split into shards, splinters, or flat sheets with sharpened edges. Many of the Peakerfolk, those who had survived the crushing rocks remain in their caves. But they are hungry and some have already emerged to seek sustenance.

A figure of a boy on a high rock is silhouetted against a blush sky, out of sight to most, and only visible from the margins of the forest. A Wolfdog is at his side. The creature yawns and as its mouth opens it seems to encompass the sphere of the rising sun. Then, the jaw snaps shut. The boy's arm reaches out to stroke the length of the beast, patting the head as it nuzzles him. A thin stream of smoke rises from the rock. A few twigs and a broken branch lay across the thin flames, and the stench of burning Ruba taints the air. But with no breeze to carry the smoke away, the trail rises, up and up, until the rose-grey line becomes so slender and fine that it disappears into the pallid sky.

The boy picks the meat off the bones of a rat speared into the forked stick that he has been holding over the flames. He pushes one piece into his mouth and holds another out to the Wolfdog.

'Here, Worro,' he says, holding it above the Wolfdog's nose.

Worro snatches at the meat. As his lips retract, he displays the shiny points of the teeth, the barbed canines. Even the boy does not dare to tease the Wolfdog, his closest friend, knowing that these shreds of food would barely satisfy a bird.

'This may be the last,' says the boy, quietly, as if speaking to himself. And to Worro, 'It's you and me now, Worro. We'll have to find another way.'

The Wolfdog licks his fingers and nudges his hand to ask for more food. Barco waves him away and stands up. By now, the sky has an odd, acrid tinge. Worro rises and lifting his head he howls into the valley of Ruba tree-tops. Boy and dog are on the edge of a rock, the brink of their world.

The world of the Watterishi is all but forgotten by the Peakerfolk — so many years have passed since they ventured down through the forest to the world of lakes and rivers. The arduous journey was only undertaken by the mad, the brave, or the ill-advised, and none of those had returned. Now the old footpaths and byways have grown over becoming an impenetrable force of undergrowth and tightly packed foliage, and with the added danger of the Ruba's sticky droppings the forest is a place of great danger.

Few animals survive in the darkest shadows of the forest. The grand slimers remain, the largest of the gastropods, who, unlike the other slow moving creatures have not died out. With their vile secretions, they dissolve the rubbery textures, gaining purchase on a sheath of bark, stretching and shimmying along the far branches of a tree until they reach the sweetest leaves. These days, the forest is a place of silence but for the occasional crash of an angered Stonebear whose cave has been broached by a forceful, younger male in a claim for territory. The loser is forced to leave the cave and in the ensuing battle they can be heard slipping down the scree, bellowing their thunderous invocations in a violent remonstration. By blasting a passage through the trees by the force of their anger, the Stonebears' descent continues, halting now and again, regaining ground, and returning to lost territory, only for the whole cycle to begin again. Eventually, with all their energy depleted, the winner makes his way back up to the mountain often falling into the split-rock traps that have formed in the dense undergrowth. Sometimes, the loser is left clinging to a tree in a final hug of desperation as the ribbons of sticky Ruba wrap themselves around him in an inescapable trap.

Recently, the Peakerfolk have taken to scavenging anything they can find on the borders of the Ruba forest: rodents, snake-eggs, even the flowering lichen that stinks of rotting meat. Despite the aroma of death, the Peakerfolk have found that they can fill their stomachs with few ill effects. Best of all, the finding of the source of a buried fruit stash fills them with nutrients, and good cheer. The now extinct tribe of the Cavines had a system of burying food in safe places, sometimes in caves and dugouts but other times in deep pits. The softer fruit from the Marginlands could be preserved above the line of the tundra in the ice cold conditions, and meat would keep for a season or longer. Many of the cave places have already been discovered, but now, in this time of hunger, the search for the remaining food pits has resumed in earnest.

This was all before the Soomoon wrought its cataclysmic effects, bringing uncertainty overnight. Already the Peakerfolk were struggling to find an existence along and above the Marginlands, but now, overnight, things have worsened. Barco, along with Worro, had joined one of the crews who had formed specifically to search for the old pits. Most of the Peakerfolk are still hiding in the caves, afraid to venture out after the night of the Soomoon, waiting for the feeble threats of thunder and the last of the rolling rocks to come to a halt. But Barco is waiting at the rock to meet his crew, wondering whether they will appear, somehow knowing that they will have survived. He stubs out the fire with his foot. Sure enough he can hear Jagg, Goss, and Hind approaching along the trail, their voices echoing against the rocks. Goss is the older of the brothers, the first to appear, his face is smudged and blotched purple, possibly bruised from the tumbling rock and vegetation, but most likely, the bruises come from another source.

Jagg Torgan is the father of Goss and Hind, although the title Master would be a better description. He treats the boys as if they are there to serve him. Jagg's motto is the hungrier a boy, the harder he works. Jagg has a reputation for violence and there is no doubt that he played his part in the abhorrence that is known as the Battle of the Cavines: a war that had rumbled on for years with a brutality that few could stomach. The Cavines were not easy to oust, disappearing into the cracks of the mountains, slipping along a labyrinth of narrow passages, laying traps along the way for the Peakerfolk. Jagg was only nineteen when he was promoted to captain of a squad of boys and men; many of them old, most of them hungry and all too cold to ask questions or care for anything other than the scraps of food they received in return for their fighting skills. Furthermore, they were loaded down with packs of bearskins and weapons. Some of the heavier munitions and implements were strapped to the backs of the chained Stonebears who yowled and hollered when they were whipped.

The Cavines defended their homes as best they could and were forced to resort to brutal attacks in defence of their territory. The Peakerfolk had the upper hand. Once backed into their caves there was nowhere for the Cavines to go, and they were easily slaughtered and some were captured and enslaved. A few escaped only to roam the mountains until every one of them eventually perished. At least, it is believed by the Peakerfolk that none survived, although there are tales and suspicions that the ghost of the last Cavine still wanders the mountains, taunting every traveller with sudden apparitions, frightening those who dare to venture to the far edges of the Peaker Mountains.

Jagg had survived the wars and in the lootings he had acquired some souvenirs. These were in the form of rolls of parchment, neatly tied and labelled. He had no idea what they were as he had never learned to decipher the symbols commonly used by the Cavines, or even those of the Peakerfolk. Jagg now regrets handing the maps over to Carew the Elder, but at the time he did not know enough to interpret them. They did not take much deciphering as they turned out to be maps of the mountains that marked the Cavine routes. They were first thought to be useful for traversing the high rocks and sheer edges, but then, one day someone realised that the digit marks indicated something else, something useful to the hungry

Peakerfolk. It was springtime and the snows had melted quickly, revealing a pit of hidden food.

'Hey, Barco,' Jagg is coming up behind him now. 'Not too scared by the chase of the dark planet to come out of your hole, I see.' He slaps Barco's back.

'You mean the Soomoon,' Barco says.

Jagg glares at him and Worro leaps up and snarls. For a moment Jagg backs away, holding up a hand in mock fear.

'Stay away, old hound!' Worro looks back at Barco, scrutinizing him for instruction but Barco does not move a hand or even a finger, or utter a single word.

'Well, we won't be needing the Wolfdog on this trip,' Jagg says.

'He's coming with us.' Barco speaks as if in declaration, as if the discussion is ended.

'I don't think so, boy.' Jagg is grinning, but there is no smile about his eyes.

Jagg's fists are clenched and as they begin to rise, Worro leaps up, his paws on Jagg's shoulders, pushing him to the ground.

'Where I go, he goes.' Barco declares. 'Here!' he commands. The Wolfdog returns to Barco's side, reluctantly, his upper lip lifted, exposing the barbed canines. One flick of his master's hand and Worro would sink them into Jagg's flesh.

'You should keep that beast under control,' Jagg says, rising cautiously, watching Worro all the time. He does not look Barco in the eye.

Jagg walks over to his boys, Goss and Hind, who had been smirking under their head-muffs. Now their widened eyes are fearful as they watch Jagg. Barco and Worro might have won this time, but it will not end here.

4

Barco has known Goss and Hind since they were six or seven years old. They would sneak up to the cave where he and his mother lived and try to steal his skins that were stretched and drying in the sun. He was a year older, but already he was stronger than either of them. Once, when they tried to run away, Barco caught them and beat them so hard that they begged him to let them go. Barco had not known his own strength and they have never forgiven him, neither have they forgotten. After that they took every opportunity to taunt him, always from a safe distance, often from behind the coat tails of their adopted father, Jagg. Their natural parents had been lost on an expedition of discovery in the Mountains of Qar, when a great avalanche came, their bodies never found. The boys were orphans living on their wits when Jagg found them.

Barco has started to walk away from Jagg, but Jagg's anger soon overcomes him, tempered by the only fear he feels, that of the Wolfdog.

'Come back here!' Jagg shouts at Barco, his voice husky with fury.

Despite Jagg's success as a soldier, or maybe because of it, he never settled into home life and before long his restlessness gave way to the violence of a domestic kind. Women feared him and warned their sisters and their daughters to keep away from him. His cave was the largest in the system, and despite the fact that some families had ten or more children to house and feed, he'd never shown any compassion to those in need, it was not known to be one of his characteristics.

Jagg throws his spear into the snow. The Wolfdog leaps as it hits a rock, twanging, the echo reverberating through the air. Barco stops. He turns around. He walks up to Jagg. Worro is at his side. Now Barco and Jagg are face to face: Barco, his hair falling over his shoulders, half tied back, his eyes a clear blue, and Jagg, deep lines scored into his cheeks, coarse hair from a pitted chin, narrowed eyes with only the glimmer of dark pupils. The spear has fallen on its side, an arrowhead of bone whittled into a double barb. Barco picks it up from the glistening snow.

'I think this is yours,' he says, holding it out to Jagg.

They set off in silence to follow one of the old Cavine routes, the ones that run along the edge of the Ruba forest and disappear into the thick foliage. Sometimes they have found a pit that contains enough fruit to feed twenty people for a month plus a few sides of meat, but that is rare and becoming scarcer these days, and many suspect that some of the pits were ransacked before they reached them.

The four of them speak in whispers, looking from side to side as they trek. There are dangers: the Cavine routes are used by the Stonebears. After several hours, Jagg stops. He pulls out a map and points to a place on the ground.

'There,' he says, 'about ten spade lengths down.'

They are at a place framed by towering rocks, and as they look around them, they hear the yowl of the Stonebears in the distance.

Worro howls.

'Shush, Worro.' Barco pulls the Wolfdog close to him, holding him until he is quiet.

They are in a narrow ravine in the split rock of the mountainside. A better trap could not be hewn.

'Are you sure it's here?' Goss asks Jagg.

Jagg does not answer straight away; he simply glares at the three of them.

30

'Well, what are you waiting for?' he finally says. 'Start digging.'

He throws a sharp spade-cutter into the ground and walks towards a protruding rock. He sits down, his legs crossed, his eyes closed.

Barco, Goss, and Hind throw off their jerkins and roll up the sleeves of their shirts. Their spades hit rock after rock and the clang of metal on stone echoes as it rings out across the mountain. Hind looks nervous. The last thing they need is to attract the attention of the Stonebears or the wild Wolfdogs. Worro wanders around sniffing the ground.

'Hurry up!' Jagg commands.

The weight of the snow becomes heavier the longer they dig, slinging each spadeful of icy earth to one side, revealing nothing at first. Eventually, fresh snow falls into the pit, and as it does, it turns pink. Could this be a trove of buried fruit? They glance up at the sky, most likely they are wondering if it is a reflection of the moon so soon after the Soomoon. Finally, the ground turns darker, a deeper red, and then purple. Jagg tells them to stop. He comes forward and bends down, cautiously reaching into the pit. The tiny ovals disintegrate in his hands as he lifts them out: the skins of the fruit are no longer intact, they have frozen and thawed in the freak episodes of ground warming, become slush and freezing again, leaving mere stains in the soil. All the berries have gone, absorbed into the ground, kept hidden beneath a covering of snow and ice.

5

The night before, the Peakerfolk had watched the Soomoon from the mouths of their caves, high in the mountains. They saw the full moon and then they saw the grey planet of Ares. And then the storms began and the mountains seemed to creak and rock as the winds and the rains blasted against their homeland. When the shuddering of the rocks finally relented, and the last boulders had slipped down the scree the Peakerfolk, who had crept deeper into their caves, were shivering under their hair blankets until they fell into bouts of fitful sleep. They had seen how the Soomoon was wrecking the valleys below and they knew that the river beds would be filling and swelling. Many dreamed of cursed waters, oozing and luring them to their deaths. In their sleep, they fought through suckers and winding roots that hung in long fibrous tentacles along cave walls, all the while clutching at their sleep-heavy limbs.

'See the mist rising through the trees,' Dorca says, staring out through the narrow gap in the cave entrance the following afternoon. 'Do you think we are safe now?' she asks her father.

They have not yet dared to go outside their cave for fear of falling rocks and the uneasy feeling that the waters might rise to meet them, high though they are. The storm that followed the Soomoon had lashed the mountaintops, glazing the snowline with a pink icy glow before it moved down into the valleys, throwing the land of the Peakerfolk into a strange stillness.

'Of course, nothing can penetrate the Ruba Forest.' Carew's voice is soothing, perhaps a little too assured. 'The waters will never rise beyond the trees. The mountain is still now. All is quiet. There is nothing to fear, I promise.'

'But the Soomoon. It was so...' Dorca shudders at the memory of the blazing moon as it was chased across the sky, looming larger and larger, seeming to come so close to their homeland. She rubbed her ears at the memory of the rumblings and the high whistle of the swirling winds. How they had clung to the back of their cave in fear of the boulders that were skittering past the entrance; how the air compressed, stifling them.

'Hush,' Carew says. 'It's over now. See how the lights have diminished.' Carew coughs. 'Come now, I have made some food.'

He lifts the spoon from the bowl and offers the thin soup to Dorca. She shakes her head.

'I cannot eat,' she says. 'Not now.'

'You must eat a little or you will weaken.'

'We must go to the Gathering Chamber,' Dorca says.

'All in good time. Eat this first, and then we will go.'

'But some folk will be there already,' Dorca says. 'I have seen them walking by, moving in that direction, and they have not returned.'

Carew's shoulders sink, and his head is bowed.

'They will want you to be there,' Dorca says. 'They will be expecting you. You know that. It is your duty.'

Carew looks into the trusting eyes of his daughter. If only he knew what could be done. If only he knew what could save them.

'I will go,' he says. 'But what can I say to people who are hungry and cold, or who have lost their caves in the storms, or worse, they might have lost their loved ones?'

'There must be something,' Dorca says. 'Help me down. I am coming with you.'

With her arms around her father's shoulders, she inches forward. Carew lifts her and half carries, half drags her, towards the cave entrance. She has been unable to walk since last year, and Carew is not as strong as he was, the lack of food has weakened him.

The sled is by the entrance. Once Dorca is installed, she can clip the harness around her waist and pull up the bearskin. Carew will pull the sled with his daughter on it.

Outside, the air is chilled. The stars can be seen in the late day sky looking as if they are suspended in a jelly-like fluid. They appear to be swaying, forwards and back. All is strangely clear after the storm. There are several Peakerfolk out along the track and Carew and Dorca join a long parade going in the same direction. Carew must have time to think before he arrives at the Gathering Chamber. He pulls his fur hat over his eyes, but he is noticed.

'Carew, Carew!' one man shouts as they pass by him on the sled. 'We come to hear your words.'

Carew nods but does not reply. They continue, watching the rising vapours and the snaking pink mists that lick the tops of the Ruba trees below them.

6

The Gathering Chamber is full when they arrive. The atmosphere bristling, some voices are high pitched, almost feverish. Others are quieter, more furtive, their faces pale and drawn in the low light, but their pallor is due to hunger. Barco's crew, who have been out during the day along with some of the other food-pit crews, have returned empty-handed. Barco has come to the meeting, Worro, as always, at his side.

Carew carries Dorca on his back to the front of the hall where he sets her down on a bench. There is a hush as Carew steps up onto the staging. Then silence.

Carew coughs and tries to speak but at first no words arrive.

'The time has come,' he announces finally, but he does not continue.

The faces are turned towards him, questioning, voices rumble.

'The time has come for what?'

'The time for advice?'

'The time for good counsel?'

'Show us that our leader is worthy of his position!'

They all roar.

Once the noise has subsided, Carew looks from person to person, from left to right, as if taking in the fibre of their souls. He waits. Then he swallows, focussing on each and every person in the chamber. He slowly reveals his plan — the one that is only just at that moment forming in his mind.

'We need a volunteer,' he says. 'Somebody who is willing to venture down the mountainside, to go through the Ruba Forest.'

The audience are pursing their lips, looking doubtful. All are wondering what it is he has in mind for this volunteer. All eyes are cast downward, fearful that they will be chosen.

'We have no option,' Carew continues. 'The chances are, there will be nothing left. But on the other hand, we may find something, some hope.'

The audience are silent, waiting for him to continue.

Carew looks at each of them again. 'The valley might have been swept away in the storm, but we must try. There might just be a chance, a chance that we find food, a place where we can grow food, a place that is more fertile than this barren mountain.'

His audience is looking up at him as if trying to absorb the meaning of his words.

'We won't know unless we try,' he continues, his voice quieter. 'Unless, someone is willing to go down there.'

Single voices can be heard from the general rumbling.

'It'll be certain death to the volunteer.'

'The forest is too dangerous.'

'And then there's the Watterishi — if any have survived — they won't have forgotten, they will be waiting to kill us.'

'None of us are strong enough to volunteer. We're too weak, too hungry.'

The level of noise from the gathering is gaining in force. Carew lifts his hand for silence.

'There might be somewhere at the lower edges of the forest,' he says. 'Somewhere fertile, somewhere that is not swamped with water, where we can grow our crops, and set our traps.

'It's our last chance,' Carew states, loudly, 'our only chance.'

'No one who has ever set out for the land of the Watterishi has come back,' an old woman in the front row says. 'Not since the rise of the great Ruba forest all those years ago. We can't sacrifice our children; our sons and grandsons. It isn't right.'

'Does anyone else have a better suggestion?' Carew asks. His question lingers in the air.

A man climbs up onto a bench. It is Doon, a planter, a farmer, a maker of traps; a pragmatist.

'We must work together to gather in the soil, as much as we can,' he says. 'There might still be good soil in the margin lands below the mountains but before the Ruba forest begins; places we haven't discovered. If we work to gather the soil, we can plant our seeds.'

'And where will the seed come from, Doon?' Carew looks at him, keeping his gaze steady. 'Have we not already eaten the seed? And where do hungry people get the energy to work the soil? No. There is nothing to sustain us. There is nothing left.'

Doon continues. 'There must be other places in the mountains, ones we have yet to discover.'

'All the mountains as far as we can see from Peaker Height have been mapped,' Carew continues.

'There is the North,' Doon insists, 'where no one goes, to Qar, and beyond.'

A shudder runs through the crowd, all are in fear of Qar. It is a place of darkness and death, and beyond Qar is only the abyss of the unknown. Doon is pulled from his bench and back into the crowd.

'We have put all our efforts into trying to survive and now the end is coming,' Carew says. 'The last sign came with the Soomoon.'

It was true that many folk had almost died of starvation, others had succumbed to the blight of disease. Some stayed within the dark interiors of their caves, believing that the light of sun and moon drew away their energies. But their skin became pallid, their limbs weak. Carew's daughter, Dorca, had been one of the unfortunate ones. She had fallen ill, weakening it seemed, at the wane of each moon. At first she was merely tired, but even with long periods of rest, after many moons she seemed to have no strength at all. Carew believed he would lose his daughter but eventually Dorca regained some of her vitality, although she had lost the ability to walk, and the Peakerfolk knew of no cure.

'You know as well as I that there is only the swamplands of the old Watterishi tribes left,' Carew continues. 'Maybe we will find more Wingfish.'

'They are hardly worth their weight in bones,' someone near the front says. 'The few we have left are hardly able to breed.'

The Peakerfolk warriors who had defeated the Watterishi in their last encounter had returned to the mountains with souvenirs: a few Wingfish slipped into water-filled pouches. Many of the Wingfish expired before they reached the mountains but a few had survived the journey and were placed in a great cavern lake. At first, they were cared for and given sustenance from the supply of Gringrows that had been brought with them, but eventually this had diminished and the Peakerfolk had not found an adequate substitute for the curly greens. The Wingfish were forced to feed on the silt floor of the caverns, living off the small amount of plant matter and tiny creatures that survived there; subsequently their bodies became thin and translucent. The Wingfish had their wings clipped so that they could never escape from the caves and many of them died. The few that carried on and bred provided a meagre source of food for the Peakerfolk. But mainly they provided entertainment for the mountain folk who liked to watch the more energetic

Wingfish race from one end of the underground lake to the other, the Peakerfolk placing bets on which one would get to the other side first.

Carew's face is drawn and pale, the bones of his cheeks show white through his flesh.

'If we stay here, we'll starve to death. We must take this risk, there's no other way.'

The crowd is agitated, their voices are grating one against the other, questions surface, fears arise:

'No one has gone down there since the end of the Watterishi Wars.'

'If they tried, no one has ever come back alive.'

'Carew is right.'

'Carew is wrong.'

'We must go there and take back the land from the Watterishi.'

'But who would be mad enough to enter the Ruba forests?'

'Such a plan is certain death.'

'What good will it do the rest of us?'

Finally, a man steps forward, his face cannot be seen beneath the grey cowl. His voice is high-pitched, nasal, as if in an attempt to disguise it. 'I have the answer,' he says. 'We must look to the old ways.'

There is a rumble of curiosity, all are ready to listen.

'We must sacrifice our best Wolfdog, sprinkle its blood on the ground,' he says. 'Then perhaps our seasons will be fruitful again.'

There is a great intake of breath throughout the crowd. Wolfdogs are sacred to the Peakerfolk. They are never killed for their meat or for any reason. In years gone by, when the young men had gone to the valleys to fight the Watterishi, the Wolfdogs had remained with the women and children as guards of the caves or the pullers of sleds.

After the battles they had been honoured for their protection and a promise made that their service would be remembered always and that they would never be dishonoured or harmed. The older generation of Peakerfolk consider that to sacrifice a Wolfdog is the worst, the most brutal, uncivilised of acts.

Everyone is looking towards a place at the centre of the hall — towards Barco's feet. Worro, the sleek-coated Wolfdog, the largest of his breed, lays at his master's side, unaware that he is in danger. The two are inseparable — as Barco's foot shifts, so too does Worro's. Barco puts out his hand, grabbing onto the loose skin around the Wolfdog's neck.

'No!' Barco shouts. 'Never! I will never allow it.'

Before the crowd can turn towards him, Barco lets out a sharp whistle. The crowd automatically make way, opening a channel for the young man and his Wolfdog. Unseen by most, the man in the cowl turns to his friend and whispers into his ear. Barco and Worro break into the chill atop the silent mountain, striding away from the Gathering Hall, leaving the voices behind them. For a moment the crowd behind them are silent and then a slow wall of sound rises from the gathering.

7

The night has been long and cold and when dawn arrives, the land is filled with a blood-coloured light, the muddy waters have found new passageways, new inlets and the lives of the Watterishi are like the detritus floating and falling into the dark waters. The primo Wingfish lies on a slop of silt where the river has retreated. His blue light, the mark of his sting, is diminishing, second by second, until it is extinguished in the slip of the mire. The dwellings of the Watterishi are gone: the only trace are the stumps of their posts in the mud.

Maysun awakes, coughs, vomits a slick of mud, tries to stand, and then stumbles and slips onto the bank. She is face down. She is covered in the thick brown slime that surrounds her. The hut is — but there is no hut. She does not recognise the land around her. She has been swept downstream and now she must return. She does not know how much time has passed.

She must find Omma, Pa, the others. Where are they? She doesn't know which way to go so she watches the way the water runs and starts to walk along the bank upstream. She slips and falls with every other step. She cries out but her voice is swallowed by the constant rushing of water from all directions. She hunkers by a pool, washes the dirt from her face, swills around her mouth, drinks a little of the earthy water. From here she looks all around, trying to find her bearings in the flattened land. Nothing is familiar.

All around her is mud, slipping and sliding and oozing. Everything has been suffocated by the slimy earth. Even the Ruba trees at the edge of the forest, in the distance, have lost their footholds and their white roots are exposed, flapping in the running waterways. The rivers and the lakes have all widened and melded one into another. There is no path towards the lakes of the East, no lakes exist, only oceans of water. If anyone survived they would not recognise the place and could only assume that they have been lifted and floated to another place far, far away. Nothing is as it was. The only sounds are the bubbles popping like the opening mouths of fish as they reach the surface, leaving circles, rings, temporary scoops on the surface.

Before her, the mud is rising, but only a little. There is a swelling, a burgeoning of silt. And then there is a parting and a sucking as whatever lies beneath begins to rise. It is pushing upwards as if reaching for the sky, or the air. The mud slips to reveal the back of a hand, the arm and the flesh are uncovered and the hump is rising and swelling, forming a back. Maysun can make out the spine, the ribs that are spread out on either side and she knows that someone is there, beneath the surface of the mud. For a moment she is frightened, scared of what might emerge, but then she realises that it is a person, a Watterishi, and she rushes to help them up, to pull them above the surface. But the slurping and gasping continues. She pulls at the shoulders until the body is upright, sitting forward, the legs thrown out in a wide V, the chin fallen onto the chest, the mud dripping down, slopping around the thighs. It is a man but she cannot make out the shape of the face let alone recognise him. The eyes are closed, lids heavy with mud, the features dulled by the slick. The only clue as to who this might be, is the sack strapped around the waist. It has split open and its contents are oozing from within: Gringrows, trails of curly Gringrows, and a circle, a flat piece of glass.

'Pa? It's you, isn't it?' she cries.

Maysun pushes the mud away from his face with her

fingers, her thumbs gently wiping across the eyelids; she tries to pull him upright, shakes him, but he only slumps forward. She slaps him to encourage his breath, but her own hands slip away and a single bubble rises from his mouth as he slips from her grasp.

She tries to catch hold of him once more but the bog is deep and strong. She cries out, yet it is no good. Pa is already disappearing below the surface, his cold body soon to be embalmed in the mud. She will be pulled in too if she does not let go. She grasps at the slimy earth, but it is too late. He is being sucked away from her.

'Come back, Pa,' she begs, but it makes no difference. The circle of mud that surrounded Pa has closed around him, releasing a sigh like a mouth after the final swallow. He has disappeared and she is alone. The piece of glass sparkles amidst the muddy Gringrows that have escaped the sack and she picks it up and holds it for a moment before she hugs it to herself. Then her tears begin to fall. She begins to wail as her cries and her tears mingle with the mud. 'I'm sorry,' she says. 'Pa, I am so sorry. I said the word... it was me.' She shakes her head as if in disbelief, full of guilt. 'I have destroyed everything.'

She sinks to the ground, at first not caring that she is sinking. And then she panics as she tries to move forward. She rolls from side to side but she is being sucked further into the mud. She tries to get up but the mud will not let her go. Finally, with all her might she propels herself forward, and stumbling and falling, she makes her way towards a bank with a stony edge. There is a crack in a rock that is wide enough to take her hand and she is just able to drag herself up onto a ledge. She lays on the rock, buries her face in her hands and weeps.

Maysun is on a promontory that juts out into the water-filled valley. Perhaps this is the lake where she came with Pa to collect the Gringrows, now misshapen with flood water. She stands up, looks all around.

'Kiri quar kiri,' she calls. The words ring out across the razed land. And again. Louder. 'Kiri quar kiri!'

Her voice rebounds, echoing around the valley, ululating, rising higher and higher with every call. Her words are carried beyond the valley, beyond the trees, higher than the mountains, vibrating around the rocks until it finally disappears in the humming of the sky. There is no return this time, no echo, and all is silent. Maysun closes her eyes. She is bereft, lost in the only world she knows.

But then, a change. The air is filling with tiny sounds: titterings, plockings. It is the clicking of Wingfish, and the girl who stands on a single rock that protrudes into a waterlogged valley listens, straining to hear the sounds. She points her finger towards the horizon where the brown water meets the pink sky. There is a hush, a silence that is so intense that it could be mistaken for a sudden loss of hearing, a deafness brought on by the change in atmosphere. But the waters are beginning to move, swirling gently at first, and then as if a thousand pinching fingers are plucking the surface, there is a multiplicity of eruptions and the waters part, opening in pockets as far as the eye can see, and from within each pocket a dozen Wingfish rise. The girl's finger moves, slowly, drawing an infinite loop, and as the fish rise into the air, they reflect the shape of the figure she is drawing in the air. She calls again and points up and down and in every direction. The Wingfish rise to her command, drop to her call, shimmer with the tones of her voice, swooping and falling, simultaneously.

8

Every Peakerfolk has come to the Gathering Chamber to answer the call to a rarely summoned Total Meeting: the women, children, men; all muffled within their bearskins. They have brought their Wolfdogs with them too. They have been there for many hours, waiting, wondering what will happen. Will someone come forward? A volunteer to make the dangerous trek through the Ruba Forest to the land of the Watterishi.

The hall is packed and the atmosphere thick with tension. The Peakerfolk stand together, cloak to cloak, jostling to get nearer to the front. They are here, again, to listen to Carew, the quiet and sometimes reluctant leader. They want a decision. Now. They have had it with discussions, with arguments, with the speeches from the self-interested. They don't even want a new leader. They want action.

Carew is standing on the platform — a stage made from the wood of a storm branch. It was erected in the days of plenty when there was even time to carve furniture or draw, or paint pictures on the walls of the caves. But all that has gone, replaced only with the ache of hunger.

Carew holds up his hand.

'Someone called to see me last night, after the last gathering. A person who came to offer his service to us all.'

They all look around, at their neighbours, at the crowd, frowning, questioning, wondering. Carew continues.

'This brave fellow Peakerfolk has volunteered to go down into the valley through the perilous Ruba Forest to seek out a new place for us to settle, to build new homes.'

Carew beckons to Barco, who has been standing at the

end of the front row, unnoticed, his Wolfdog at his side. As he steps forward Carew takes hold of his hand, and with triumph, lifts it into the air. A cheer goes up. Everyone is looking at Barco, some have tears in their eyes, some are smiling, some are chanting his name. But somewhere in the crowd, at the back of the hall, there is a man with a hood half covering his face who is not cheering. Instead he is nodding to each of the young men at his side.

Carew draws Barco towards him, then he turns to the audience, holding up one hand to silence them. Before he speaks, a voice comes from the back of the chamber.

'If Barco goes, then we go too.' It is Goss. 'Yes,' concurs his brother. 'We go too.'

They are pushed forward by the hooded man between them. Barco looks at Carew, questioning, confusion in his eyes but Carew can do nothing. He knows that the crowd will want as many volunteers as are keen to go. Barco's face becomes paler, and his jaw has the flicker of a muscle. He remembers how during the recent winter snow-blitz Jagg and his boys survived by stealing from others, and by killing the bear cubs and eating their meat raw. Worro is also wary: he bares his teeth and growls. Those in the front row stand back, afraid he will leap at them.

But the crowd are delighted. The room has erupted with applause and cheers. Barco is swept away from the stage to join the others. Now there are three heroes. The Peakerfolk lift them high into the air and carry them around the room for everyone to reach out and touch. Promises are made: they will be given food (what little there is), they will be given skins and water carriers. Those who have nothing, give only their blessing.

Soon, everyone has left the hall, and the young volunteers leave to prepare for their journey. They have the rest of the day and the night ahead of them. Barco and

Worro slip away leaving the others. Barco wants nothing to do with Goss and Hind. Let them spend their last evening celebrating their popularity. Jagg will certainly make the most of it, greedily consuming all the gifts of food and drink, meagre though they might be.

Barco is determined to set off on the assignment alone. Carew and the good Peakerfolk have placed their faith in him, and he will not let them down. He will travel lightly, carrying only a small sack and his bow and quiver on his back. He will set off early the next day, intending to make his provisions last, finding as much food as he can on the way. He knows the upper reaches of the forest that border onto the Marginlands, the areas of thin trees that protrude according to the fall of the land and the soil, and he knows the tracks made by the falling bears, the ones that will lead him into the deeper parts of the forest. There is no point in packing more than is necessary as everything will swell in the steamy atmosphere and become heavier. He wants to avoid being dragged into the morass of bogs and treacherous roots. Everyone knows that in recent times, anyone who has ventured into the Ruba Forest has failed to return.

On the last night in his cave, Barco listens out for the sounds of the Marginlands: the creatures that scurry into their hidings avoiding the trap of the sticky Ruba roots and the tiny birds who dwell amongst the topmost trees. When he thinks about the journey ahead, without the company of Worro, in truth he is fearful. He can hardly bear the thought of his first task the next day.

9

As Barco is falling asleep he hears a rustling sound. Perhaps it is the dry leaves in the wind, but in his half-sleep he dreams that the Ruba trees are rising, they are lifting their roots from the ground and slowly, they move forward, marching up the mountain, dragging their trunks across the Marginlands until they reach his cave. He hears them calling to him, reaching out to him in his sleep. As they surround him, he feels the heat from their trunks, and he breaks out into a sweat. He cannot breathe and now he is bursting out of a deep pool in the forest. He shudders and shivers as he wakes. He holds his breath but there is nothing but the silence of the dark and the thump of his own heart.

Night passes. As the cave walls flicker with the grey light of dawn, Barco's hand drops along the side of the bed. He waves his hand, feeling for the head and the ears of the sleeping Worro. Satisfied with a warm lick, he turns over and sleeps a little longer.

When the sunlight is facing the mountain Barco emerges from his cave with Worro at his heel. Across the stone step at the entrance of his cave he finds a circle of twigs. They are tied together and crossed in the centre: six spokes, each end inserted into the bent circle of the soft wood circumference. The Wolfman has visited.

Tears loosen from Barco's eyes as he hunkers down and gathers up the Wolfman's gift. Beside him is his loyal hound. As he whispers into his ear, Worro shakes his head as if not wanting to feel his master's breath or to understand the words that come from his lips. Instead, he licks the tears, nuzzling against Barco.

'Come on, Worro,' Barco says quietly. 'It's time to go.'

The Wolfdog looks uneasy at the choked sound of his master's voice, and he growls as if responding to a threat.

Barco scans the forest. A line of mist is rising from the trees. He looks at the cave and the forest below. He knows that soon he will be making his way across the stony margins, following the line of the forest of Ruba, along the Marginlands, until he comes to the opening of an old Cavine track. He will follow it as far as it goes, and slip away into the forest. He watches for a few moments, knowing that he might never return, then he slowly turns and walks further up the mountain, calling to Worro.

Together they walk to Carew and Dorca's cave, Worro's head nudging and butting against Barco's knee. Barco knows that Dorca is the only one who understands Worro and she will be sure to take good care of him. And Worro will be a help to her.

'Come on,' he calls to Worro. 'It'll be fine. I'll be back for you, I promise.' But Worro's head drops lower and his pace slackens.

Dorca's mother was a friend of his mother's and Barco has always felt that Dorca and Carew are the nearest thing he has to a family. Barco's mother had been shunned by the community and forced to bring up her only son on the margins, outside the rest of the community. Barco never understood what terrible humiliation had befallen his mother. He only felt her pain and heard her tears in the darkest hours of the night. She would never speak of the past. If ever Barco asked about his father, she would explain that he need only know that his father had once been a good man, but that sometimes even good men change. In any case, his mother claimed, she had always wanted to return to the Marginlands of her early life, but Barco suspected more and more that they were living in a state of hiding rather than retreat.

Then, she had fallen ill, suddenly, from dawn to dusk she had gone from good health to poor. It was only after she had died that Barco heard the whisperings. It happened at the same time as other Peakerfolk had become sick. Many believed that a disease had fallen from the sky because the first symptoms had shown themselves soon after a great meteor shower.

Barco had tried to treat his mother with herbs and poultices using all the knowledge that he had gained from her, but there was little that helped. His mother had learned her trade from her mother and many times she had saved the lives of others. The Peakerfolk came to her in the dead of night, shawled and covered lest anyone should recognise them. They were always very grateful for her tenderness, and they thanked her and repaid her in kind, but they would never be seen to visit in the light of day. And he was left watching as her life force ebbed away. Their only friend had been the old Wolfman. As ancient as the crags and as rugged, the Wolfman dwelled in a place that no one could ever find. Barco and his mother believed he must live among the Wolfdogs, and so they called him The Wolfman. He would appear and then, just as quickly, he would disappear. He wore a cloak of leaves and a mask of lichen.

Sometimes, Barco would find leaves tied with a piece of stringy bark outside their cabin door. Once he found twigs, twenty or thirty of them, laid out in pairs and threes on the ground outside their cave. 'The Wolfman has been,' Barco's mother exclaimed. Another time, Barco found a bunch of stems that had been tied together with a sinew of a vine. The twigs still held their green leaves. His mother looked at the broad leaves, dripping with stream water, and she held them under her nose. 'These are the leaves of the Lammerherb,' she had said. Her eyes lit up. 'I haven't seen these for many years. I wonder where he found them.' The boiling of the leaves filled the cabin with a fragrant scent.

Most Peakerfolk had never seen the Wolfman, and those who had feared his wild eyes that could be seen through the slits of his lichen mask. Many warned their children to keep away. But Barco wasn't frightened of the Wolfman. Once, the Wolfman appeared before Barco as he was setting a trap. The old man was cradling something in his arms, crooning a tuneless song, feeding scraps of meat into the mouth of a creature. Barco went up to him. He had never been this close before, and he could smell the damp moss and see the cracks in the lichen face and the green growths of delicate branches that wavered from his head. The Wolfman continued crooning and feeding the tiny mouth until Barco was close by, and then he looked up, straight into the eyes of the boy. 'For youeth, for youeth,' he had said. And he held the animal out. 'For youeth, Worro, Worro.'

The Wolfman had pushed the Wolfdog puppy into Barco's arms. Barco shrieked as the arrow-sharp teeth pierced the flesh of his finger.

But the Wolfman simply retreated, disappearing with a hiss, a stream of notes that lingered in the air before dissipating leaving only a dissonance that haunted and echoed in Barco's mind.

10

Goss and Hind are awake. The sun is high in the sky. In fact, almost a whole day has passed since they took up the challenge to accompany Barco on his mission to seek out a new land for the Peakerfolk beyond the Ruba Forest.

'Hey, what's going on?' Hind asks, rubbing his head.

Goss is sitting on Hind's bed.

'What's happening?' Goss asks. 'Don't you remember, idiot.'

'I remember that someone volunteered,' Hind's voice is fuzzy as he cowers under the bedding, 'to go to the land of the Watterishi, but…'

'Yes, that was Barco.' Goss is laughing. 'And you and me. So come on, let's start packing.'

'I can't go today,' Hind points out.

'And why would that be?'

'I promised Jagg I'd skin the Stonebear.'

'I'm sure that can wait, dear brother.'

'But he'll be expecting me.'

'There's no getting out of it now,' Goss states.

They are silent as they both remember Postra who had been so brave, so strong. And yet, even he had never returned from the Ruba forest.

'Well, maybe we could let Barco go first, and, if he survives… you know, we could follow him.'

'It's true we need to keep a close eye on him.' Goss sighs. 'Following him isn't such a bad idea.'

'Full of ideas, me,' says Hind, looking pleased with himself. He sits up and begins to pull on his clothes.

'But first we need to find him,' Goss says. He gets up and groans. Now it's his turn to rub his head. 'This is all your fault. You shouldn't have opened that last flagon.'

'You told me to,' says Hind, standing up, pulling on his trousers.

'Come on,' Goss says. 'You can bet he won't be waiting around for us, you can be sure of that.'

Once they are both dressed, they stumble around the cave pushing clothes and food into their sacks, stuffing grainy flatbreads into their mouths. Finally they emerge into the midday air, blinking and cursing. They set off, stumbling along the track that leads towards Barco's cave.

'Barco!' Goss shouts into the cave entrance. 'Come on now, Barco, it's time for our little adventure.'

The two brothers enter the cave. It is sparsely furnished but tidy, unlike their own. Quietly they shuffle over to the bed.

'He's still sleeping,' Hind whispers.

Then he laughs, but it is more of a hiss. Goss grabs him and points to a chamber pot. Hind understands what he must do, and he picks it up and tiptoes towards the sleeping Barco. Goss shoves him in the back just as his full hands are hovering over the bed and the basin slips, emptying its pungent content over the bedclothes. The bulge in the covers has flattened. The smell of urine fills the air.

'He's gone,' Goss spits. 'He's tricked us.'

They go outside, and muttering curses, they haul their loads onto their backs and set off towards the forest. They are only a short way from Barco's cave when Goss hunkers down and points to the ground.

'That's our prey,' he says.

The soft soil is impressed with footprints, raw and fresh on the ground, marks that tell of the stitched sole of a Peakerfolk shoe. There can only be one who might pass this way — Barco.

11

Barco has beaten his way through the tangled woody edge of the Marginlands and descended the mountain towards the thickest part of the Ruba forest. There have been two sundowns since he left the mountain, and another quickly approaching. He is glad that he remembered to sharpen the blade of the old iron sickle; it has served him well, cutting and slicing his way down through the mountainside of dense undergrowth.

He can see little of the sky now, as the canopy of the trees has grown thick and lush. In any case, it is the end of the day and the light is leaving; the shadow of the mountain darkens the already deep green of the forest. Underfoot the ground is getting stickier as it does at the time of dusk.

He looks for a place to rest, but he can hardly see anything, let alone a clearing where the floor of the forest is dry enough to lie down. It is oozing with sticky sap. He looks up at the trees. Already he is feeling a sense of panic — he is in danger of suffocating or being absorbed into the ground and slowly perishing in the morass of seeping Ruba. He makes out a branch that is in reaching distance but high enough from the ground that his weight will not bend it too low. He takes his hammock, and a rope from the sack on his back and ties it around his waist and clambers onto the flattest part of the branch. Then he flings the rope around the branch and ties it, looping each end to his hammock, securing it to the tree for the night. The tree is already dripping its night secretions, and he covers his head and body with the large palmate leaves of the mountain Mannicat that he had picked further up the mountain. The solvent-like sap within the Mannicat leaves is enough to disperse the Ruba, and as the white droplets roll to the ground they sound like rain on leaves.

The next morning he emerges from beneath the Mannicat leaves. His head is aching, and his throat is throbbing from breathing the essence of the mountain leaf but at least he has been spared the Ruba secretions wrapping around him and making him into a chrysalis. He takes out the water bag from his sack and drinks deeply, he chews on some scragrat remains, and drinks some more before releasing the hammock from the tree.

Barco forces his way through the streams of sticky tree sap avoiding the stringy loops that unexpectedly fly out and entwine a wrist, or snag an ankle. He is so tired, and all he wants is to sink to the ground to rest for a moment, but he knows that if he stops, all could be lost. Within minutes he might be bound by the tendrils of Ruba and preserved in a rubber cocoon, unable to ever escape.

12

Goss and Hind chew on the last of their dried bear meat. They are lost. They have not been able to sleep at night for fear of the forest. Their water carriers lay beside them, almost empty. They are terrified that they may not find a stream to refill them.

'It's your turn to fetch the water,' Hind says to Goss, hopefully.

'Unless you want to do it, we'll wait until morning,' Goss replies, 'then we'll decide whose turn it is.'

They've heard the stories of the forests throughout their lives. They know how a river can turn out to be a mere mirage to a thirsty man like a trap primed and set to catch the unsuspecting traveller. The tale of Postra haunts them as they listen to the drip, drip of the Ruba secretions all around them. Neither speak.

'This is all your fault,' Hind declares eventually. His voice is whiny, his lower lip shaking.

'It was your idea to come this way in the first place,' Goss says.

They hear a crash behind them. There is an explosion of leaf and a cracking of branches but they see nothing. They cling on to each other until the forest becomes silent once again. When they are sure that no creature is nearby, they run, lurching forward down the hillside, skelter and helter, halting only when they can go no further. They find themselves within an eerie ring of Ruba trees, an enclosure that is more prison than forest.

Hind cries out.

'Shut up!' Goss hits him.

They are completely still, petrified, in the centre of the circular copse. They slump to the soft ground, tired, weak.

'Let's get some rest,' Goss says. 'We're probably safe here.'

They pull out the groundsheets from their packs, begin to set up their makeshift camp for the night. In the middle of the circle is a mound, the turf is coarser here, a few twigs laying crossways around the centre. Hind jumps on to it, and then looks down. He yelps. Then he lurches to one side and retches.

Goss comes over, and cautiously looks down. As he stares at the mound it takes on the form of a face.

'Postra!' Goss whispers. 'It's Postra.'

Here is their old friend, half absorbed into the earth by the forest, his head partly preserved in a rubbery slip of Ruba. The trees around them are creaking.

'Come on,' says Goss. 'Let's go.'

Goss grabs Hind, who picks up their packs, and they begin to run. Out through the circling trees, the trunks of the Ruba catching at them, running and falling, hitting the earth and dragging each other up, and on they go, further and faster until they are rolling, unable to stop, gathering leaves, and rolling on, down and down the mountainside.

13

Worro is still waiting for Barco to return. He is staring in the direction where he last saw his beloved master disappearing. Carew and Dorca have their doubts. Barco has not returned, it is too soon in any case, but there has been no sign; no signals in the rising mist. Worro paws at the door, he senses their sadness. He whines and will no longer eat the small rations of food that Dorca places before him.

'I don't know what we can do,' Carew says. 'It's like he's lost everything.'

Dorca agrees. 'He is waiting for Barco, and he won't give up, ever. He is Worro, Barco's Wolfdog.'

'Look how he moves,' Carew says. 'So slowly, with great effort and with a heavy heart.'

Carew can empathise with Worro. Since the death of Dorca's mother, a few years back, Carew has felt lonely, he has become quieter, his reactions slower, and he takes time to consider every action. Of course he cares for Dorca, more than anyone else in the Peaker world, but she looks so much like her mother and is a constant reminder of his loss.

In many ways he is a good leader. He carries out his duties with consideration, with stoicism, and without emotion. He can no longer feel the sorrow of the other folk or even their anger. It is as if he has become inured to his own pain and suffering. Perhaps this is why they seek him out to solve their problems, he muses, they want his opinion and know that he will not favour one over another. He is amused that his withdrawn nature might be taken as wisdom. For all that, he is at a loss now.

Father and daughter have fallen silent. All the words

have been spoken, the words that were in their thoughts just a moment ago. If Worro has lost his master then he and all the Peakerfolk might have lost everything too, every hope they had for a future in a new land. No one speaks of Goss and Hind knowing that it was Jagg's idea that they accompany Barco. Those boys have no real courage in their hearts and their sender has only greed. Dorca and Carew know that Barco slipped away from Goss and Hind, leaving the Mountain on his own, and they are glad.

'He wouldn't still be waiting like that if he thought Barco had gone forever,' Dorca says, hopefully.

'Wolfdogs are intelligent creatures,' Carew muses, 'and it's true that this one is special.'

Worro looks at them both, his eyes wide and questioning.

'I just wish we'd had word, anything, a sign, so that we know that Barco is still alive.'

Dorca's day chair is in the bay of the cave. From here she can see out across the span of the mountains. She can see the top edges of the Ruba forest, the sides of the snow-clad ridges. She can see the sky as it changes from day to night, the moon as it breaches the cusp of their world

'He's alive,' Dorca says, almost under her breath, as she stares out across the white wilderness. 'I know it.'

Carew puts his arm around his daughter's shoulder. 'Let's be patient, keep our hopes alive,' he says. 'That is all we can do.'

Today the forest is darker, greener, closer to them, as if the Marginlands are diminishing, and the Forest is moving up the mountain.

'I think the trees are on the move,' Dorca says.

It may be that the land where they have lived for generations is turning against them now, Carew thinks.

Perhaps they are cursed by some ill-begotten force that has turned its attention onto the Peakerfolk and wants to destroy them. Carew is disturbed when Dorca speaks of the trees. It is as if she believes they are creatures that can expand and stretch, clawing their way up the mountain: beasts determined to find their way into the foothills of the icy rock lands.

14

Barco has arrived at a place where the ground is level. The trees make way for him as if drawing apart a thick green curtain. They reveal a lake and a valley of mud — the land of the Watterishi. He looks all around and sees that the land right up to the edge of the Ruba Forest is filled with silt. He smiles and he thinks of Doon who would be delighted to see this sight. Barco knows that as long as the waters remain receded there will be plenty of soil for the Peakerfolk to grow their crops.

When the tribes of the Peakerfolk and the Watterishi first met, they were wary of each other and fell into the shadows or retreated in fear. Eventually, it was the bravery of a single person from each tribe, a woman in the case of the Watterishi, and a man from the Peakerfolk, who came face to face in the forest. Curiosity overcame them. They both spoke in languages the other could not understand but they could feel the vibrations of each other's voices and the echoes and oscillations they made through the trees. To the ears of the Peakerfolk, the language of the Watterishi formed a kind of song, singing through the air. Their languages, whether having evolved at different altitudes or coming from different parts of their vocal anatomy, made a curious harmony when they conversed.

In those days, the forests were not such a place of great danger. They were overgrown and difficult to negotiate, and there were few Ruba trees. The two tribes were able to meet half-way up the mountainside. They brought food and liquids to share and barter; sweet honeycombs of the mountains, where the sweet-nectar flowers bloomed, were exchanged for the Gringrow foods of the lands of the Watterishi.

But soon the Watterishi realised that the Peakerfolk wanted something else, something they were not prepared to part with: their sacred Wingfish. Only in times of great hunger would they allow themselves to eat the Wingfish, and then only modest amounts and with the respect like that of a holy sacrifice. They had seen what the Peakerfolk would do to them — kill them in great quantities and cook them on their open fires. So the Watterishi had caught as many of the Wingfish as they could in their nets, carefully gathering them and taking them to the parts of the valley that the Peakerfolk had not yet discovered. Some of the Wingfish remained and were prey to the mountain folk. In those days there was no one to whom the Wingfish responded — there was no Maysun.

From then on, the Watterishi became shadows that slipped among the trees, whispers in the leaves; they were hardly ever seen. The Peakerfolk believed that the Watterishi threatened them with curses and spells and whenever they came across each other in the forest, the Peakerfolk held up their weapons, shaking them, exposing their sharp-edged knives, and the Watterishi retaliated with slings and rocks. It did not take long before a battle commenced.

It was at this time, when the Watterishi and Peakerfolk were at odds with one another, when the planet of Ares came close to their own Moon and a Soomoon struck. Everything shook: the earth, the trees, the mountains; rocks shattered, the ground split open swallowing the soil and spewing up deposits of minerals that had lain dormant for years. The Ruba trees, their roots straddling the rubble, took hold of the forest and gained mastery. And that was the beginning of the great Ruba Forest.

Barco is in the valley of the Watterishi. It has taken

him a long time to get here but his journey has been unhindered by spirits or beasts or the dangers of the roots or branches of the trees, and he is thankful that Goss and Hind have not come with him. He would not be surprised to find out one day that they had been hiding in the Marginlands, fearful that the Peakerfolk would discover their cowardice. He feels sure that they could not have left the mountain before him, if indeed, they had dared to leave at all as he has seen no sign of them and heard no sound.

Barco steps forward towards a great lake, but he retreats behind a rock as he sees something or someone is moving at the edge of the water. He peers from behind the rock and sees that the surface of the lake is pocked with tiny explosions. He is watching a myriad of plump Wingfish spinning and flying, spirally around and around, and a girl who is standing at the edge waving her arms in graceful movement. The girl wears a shift made of a woven green material, the like he has never seen before. From the pocket of her tunic falls a tail of green plaited leaves that wavers as she moves. He cannot see her face, but from her clothes, he imagines that she might have come from the treetops, fallen to the ground as a leaf or seed and blossomed into a person.

Barco watches as she seems to direct the Wingfish one way and then the other. He soon realises that the Wingfish are indeed reacting to her, and that they are rising and falling to her command. She waves across with the back of one hand and then with a movement of the other, some change direction. A single finger pointing up and they follow one behind another high above the lake in a fountainous stream. Another flourish, and they shift as one, high in the air, and then back again with such velocity that the air around him is moving, a blast of breeze even ruffles the trees behind the rock. It is as if they are being swung within an invisible net.

Barco has never seen so many Wingfish or any so large and healthy. He realises that there would be enough here to feed his whole village for months or even years. The Peakerfolk still have a small school of Wingfish bred from the few that had been brought up the mountain decades ago after the final skirmishes with the Watterishi. They had their wings clipped and so Barco has never seen them fly. The Wingfish in the cavernous pool of the Mountain are pale imitations of these glorious beings.

Now, as their wings catch the light, they shower the earth with the reflections of their rainbow scales. The sound brittles the air. How does the girl have the power to do this? It is as if she has a magic pulse at the end of her finger, one that can attract or repulse the Wingfish according to her will. She is calling to them in a strange language, half song, half ululation. Barco is transfixed as the sound resonates across the valley, echoing and re-echoing. For a moment, he forgets that he is a stranger in a foreign land.

The girl turns and he sees that her skin is the colour of the earth, her eyes are bright like the sky above the mountain, pale and blue. They flash when she turns in his direction, and then, for fear of being seen, he presses in closer to the rock. He doubts that she can see him but he crouches down, sinking into the mud.

When he feels it is safe, he looks up, but she is gone. He stands up, stretches his arms as he looks all around. There are trees behind him, the lake in front, but nowhere can he see another person or any sign that they exist. The land of the valley has been swept clean of everything and everyone it seems. The Soomoon may have destroyed all apart from the girl and the fish. It is as if the thick waters have swollen and burst and swept away any settlements, boats, people, and even the soil and the vegetation, leaving only mud. His feet are sinking and fixing him into the slime; as he tries to lift one leg, it comes away with the sounds of sucking and slurping. Then he hears the click of the fish and he stops and hunkers back down behind the rock. The girl has returned.

15

There is a knock on the cave door, a muffled sound as if a small gloved hand is tapping on the wood.

'Who is it?' Carew shouts from the back of the cave, where he is mending one of the straps that has become detached from the sled.

There is no reply, just a scratching and a carrying on of the soft knocking.

Worro is tilting his head to one side, gets up on his feet, stretches out his neck and lets out a loud howl. Carew takes hold of Worro's collar and pulls him to one side before opening the door.

'Fillet of Wingfish? Whole fishies?'

Carew takes a step back. A child is holding a tray, it is strapped around his neck.

'Delicious eyes of the Wingfish, juicy and tender,' the child continues.

'Where did you get these?'

'From the Wingfish Cavern, of course,' the child says, as if it was an everyday occurrence.

'Who gave you permission?'

'It's all right, mister. No need to worry.'

'No, it's not all right,' Carew explains. 'If we eat the Wingfish now, there will be none left. Ever.'

'Well, do you want some or not?' the child asks.

Carew does not recognise the child but then there are many children he does not know, and they all look the same with their shorn heads, sunken cheeks and large eyes.

Carew lets go of Worro who, by now, has stopped howling and is sniffing at the tray, his long tongue slurping and tickling the boy's hands. The boy giggles.

'Can I take your Wolfdog out for you?' he asks. 'I'm good with Wolfdogs.'

'No,' Dorca responds quickly. 'We have promised not to let Worro go with anyone else.'

'He's just a boy,' says Carew.

'Mr Torgan says he's a good tracker,' the boy adds.

'Does he now?' Carew says, slowly. 'Well you go and tell Jagg Torgan that he's not having the Wolfdog, and he had better stop killing the Wingfish.'

16

Barco is beginning to feel cold as he continues to hunker behind the rock. He peers out wondering if he might dare to show himself. If there are other Watterishi around, then they have not come to join the girl with the Wingfish. But the fish have paused in mid-flight, momentarily, as though held by invisible threads, as if they have seen him. Then they move again, resuming their course of loops and whirls. The girl seems unperturbed as she lifts and drops her arms. Then she is pointing down, to the muddy slope that slips into the lake. The fish swoop and finally they plunge in perpendicularly to the water. Circular waves lap and spiral the surface, over and over until all the busyness is calm. Around the edges, Barco can see the tiny white curls of the root ends of the unearthed Gringrows.

'You can come out now,' the girl says. She is not looking at him, but she is staring into the deep pool.

Barco climbs onto a large stone and looks over the top of the rock. The girl has not turned around. Not for a moment, and he thinks that she is talking to herself or to the Wingfish, but they have all disappeared.

'You,' she says. 'Behind the rock.'

There is no mistaking her words, in the tongue of the Peakerfolk, although they are half-formed, her accent strange. Barco remembers the Peakerfolk elders from his childhood using a few of the old words gained from their time with the Watterishi, but he does not have the confidence to try them now.

'Hi, do you mean me?' he says, in his own language. He feels self-conscious, he can hear that his own words are hard, clipped, as is common with the Peakerfolk.

She is turning slowly towards him. Her eyes are the

shade of the pool. At the same time there is a glint and he feels a warmth, and unthreatened he steps clear of the rock.

'Are you from the mountains?' the girl asks him. 'Have you come here because...' she is hesitating and then she turns towards him, looking directly at him she speaks, 'because of the Soomoon?' The last word has been uttered so quietly as if she has dropped it from a spell. She is looking at the ground and seems to be about to cry.

'I am here to seek new places to live and to grow food. I am not here to hurt you.'

'So you are from the mountains?'

The girl stares past him. Only the edge of the forest lays behind. He hears the snap of a twig and he glances over his shoulder expecting to see the shifting of leaves, a wavering branch that has been disturbed by a clambering creature. But all is quiet.

'Do not fear me. I am alone.' As he speaks, he thinks of Goss and Hind, but, after all, he has seen no trace of them.

He walks towards the girl and notices how small she is, how her hands lay loose by her side with her fingers twitching as if she is about to command the Wingfish to rise up again. He imagines the Wingfish are waiting just below the surface of the lake, waiting for their mistress's command. But her face is so sad for one so young.

He tries hard to remember some of the words he heard spoken by the elders. He holds out both of his hands, palms up, in greeting, in a sign of peace. She begins to move towards him. He smiles, and their hands almost touch, but before they meet, she flinches. He is confused. Now there is fear in her eyes, and her body is turning as if ready for flight. Barco is puzzled. For a moment she stares at him, seemingly rooted to the spot. It is as if she has been struck, paralysed in a moment. Her eyes are wide open, and as he looks into them he sees that their colour is fading and they are becoming so pale that they are almost white. Her eyes close, and slowly she slips to the ground, collapsing onto the mud before him. It is only then that he sees the reason for her fear. An arrow protrudes from the back of her shoulder and already the blood is seeping through the arm of her tunic.

17

She is light to carry, as light as a bundle of dried leaves but strangely supple and slippery in his arms and he struggles to keep hold of her. She is still, as if lifeless, her head in the crook of his arm, but her eyes are open now, and they are fixed on him. At first, he had hidden with the girl behind the rock, scanned all around them to see where the arrow had come from, but the Wingfish had risen up in a swarm and he could see no further than the nearby bank. They had gone in the direction of the unseen archer, they had gathered by the edge of the water, buzzing and droning in anger. Now he is running into the forest as if he is being chased. The slope becomes steeper as he runs higher into the forest and he is finding it hard to continue. As he slows down a slip of glass falls from Maysun's pocket. Barco sees it but there is no time to stop to pick it up. He only knows that he must find a place of safety.

'You'll soon be safe,' Barco says, breathlessly.

She does not respond, her eyes continue to stare. Their paleness is as filmy as the surface of the lake, reflecting the cloud with tints of a blue sky. He stumbles and stops for a moment to catch his breath and to look around for a safe place for the girl in the lower edges of the forest where the Ruba trees do not completely dominate. There is a tree just a little way ahead of them, it is huge, much larger than the rest, and it is on higher ground. He decides to go to it. She seems even lighter now, as if she has withdrawn into herself, pulling the weight of her life-force inside — like a flame surrounded by melting waxen walls.

When they reach the tree Barco looks around to check that no one has followed them, nor that they are watched. Everywhere is still, there is no movement in the surrounding trees. The large tree does not have the leaves of the Ruba and it has an unusual shape, bulbous around the girth, and there is an opening, an entrance at the base. Barco places the girl on a bank of dry leaf litter.

Gathering a large stick, he moves towards the tree's entrance, goes in and finds a passageway ahead of him. He follows it cautiously, tapping ahead with the stick. The pathway winds around towards the centre as he follows the shell of the inner bark passage and finally, enters a chamber. It is a perfect place to hide. Set within the heart of the tree, a little light entering from above, the ground is clear of sticky Ruba leaves with just a gentle bed of soil.

He brings the girl inside the chamber. By now her eyes are glazed, and fluttering open and shut. He lays her on the dry floor, and tips a little water into her mouth, but she is unable to swallow. She is trying to speak.

'Omma,' she calls, 'Omma.'

'You are safe here,' Barco says. 'You are wounded, but you will heal.'

'Omma,' she calls, but her voice has become a hoarse whisper. She moans. Her eyes close and beads of sweat fall from her forehead.

'I will help you. I promise.'

Barco gently rolls the girl onto her side to study the arrow that is lodged in the fleshy part of her upper arm just below the shoulder. He takes in a sharp breath as he looks at the shaft of the arrow. He recognises the nock and the feathers of the fletching. He knows it is the work of the Torgans. So, Goss and Hind must have followed him down through the forest after all.

He breaks the arrow in half so that most of the shaft remains; it will help to guide him to the arrowhead for when he must remove it from the girl's flesh. But he knows it will not be easy, and without the healing herbs to ease her pain and fight infection the girl may succumb to an illness that can kill her.

The girl's skin is as soft and as pliant as the ears of the Wolfdog. The thought, the sudden memory of Worro crushes him for a moment, and his eyes fill with tears. He remembers the herbs that his mother used when helping an injured Wolfdog that had been caught in a trap. He decides he must leave the girl in the tree chamber to look for the healing plants. He gently covers her with his jacket and brushes the loose hair from her face and again pours a little water onto her lips. This time she coughs and chokes and then opens her mouth for more. He tips a little more water and this time she swallows.

'I will find something to help you and then I will remove the arrowhead, but for now I must leave you here,' he says.

She makes a small noise like that of an injured animal. He remembers how she made the Wingfish dance and leap and quiver with all the colours of the rainbow, glinting in the sunlight and gliding through the sky.

'I am Barco,' he says, pointing to himself. 'What's your name?' he asks.

'Maysun,' she whispers, and then she closes her eyes.

He collects a couple of bowl-like curls of loose bark that are lying in the corner of the chamber and fills them with water from his pouch, placing them at her side. He also leaves her another one of his precious water pouches.

'I will return, Maysun,' he says. 'I promise.'

He makes his way back to the entrance of the tree, and waits, peering out into the forest, cautiously leaving while there is still light.

18

Hind throws a stick into the fire. It skitters over the top sending orange sparks into the undergrowth. He turns to Goss.

'You said that we'd get to the land of the Watterishi, and everything would be all right. And that we would find treasure,' he says.

Goss is sullen. 'Things don't always work out how you expect.'

Goss takes a stick and draws it across the forest floor, holding it ham-handedly. He draws incomplete circles that he scores through and stabs at the places where the intersections meet as if each mark has some special meaning.

'What are you up to now?' Hind asks. 'Sorcering?'

Something flicks up into the air with the last hit of Goss's stick, then it bounces along the ground and lands in front of Hind. Hind looks down. It is as if a tiny pool of water has fallen onto the ground, but unlike water, instead of sinking into the soil, it stays as it is, like a slip of ice. He stares at it for a moment and then looks up into the trees. There is no gap, nowhere for the light of the sky or the stars to penetrate. Goss stands up and walks around to where Hind is, looking at the slip of ice from different angles.

'What are you doing?' Hind asks.

Goss says nothing. He bends down and picks up the ice-like slice. He holds it up in front of him and then tilts it towards the ground and then up towards the trees. It does not melt in his hand. Finally, he places it over his eye and laughs.

'The trees are moving,' he says. 'They are getting

bigger, they must be growing very quickly.' He is shouting now and waving his other arm around. 'But now they are shrinking. So small. I have made them tiny.'

'Don't be ridiculous,' Hind says. 'Trees don't change like that. They take a long time to grow and they only get smaller when they're cut down.'

But Goss is laughing louder and louder, becoming hysterical.

'This is it!' he declares, and now he is jumping up and down and jigging around the fire in a dance. 'This is the treasure.'

'It doesn't look much like treasure to me,' Hind says.

'It is magic treasure!' Goss exclaims. 'And it is trying to tell us something, something from the past or, or... maybe it is from the future. Yes! I can see into the future.'

'Give it here,' Hind says. 'Come on, let me see.'

Goss passes it to him and grins as Hind holds it close to his eye.

'Hey, what's this?' Hind says. 'The trees have gone. They're just burnt stumps on the ground. And the sky is grey.' Hind is talking loudly, almost shouting.

'Shut up!' Goss says, and he looks around at the darkening forest. 'Someone might hear you.'

'There's smoke too. Everywhere. Look, the forest is on fire.'

'No, it's not,' Goss says sternly, pulling the ice piece away from Hind. 'It's just what you see in the ice. Don't you realise it's not real. It's not even ice.'

'Now I can hear something, someone is coming,' Hind whispers.

'It's the water running in the stream, you idiot.'

Goss has taken the eyeglass away from his brother and slipped it into his pocket.

They return to the fireside but they are restless,

throwing more and more twigs and small branches into the flames.

'You didn't have to kill the girl,' Hind says quietly.

'I should have got Barco,' Goss says. 'One clean shot would have been all that was needed. No one would ever have found out.'

'But he might have seen us,' Hind says.

'I don't think so, but he'll recognise the arrow that hit the girl,' Goss states. 'Whether he knows or not, it doesn't matter. We can't go back until Barco is dead. Or Jagg will kill us.'

'Those Wingfish were scary, they were angry with us,' Hind says. 'When they flew towards us like that, I really believed that they wanted to kill us.'

'How can Wingfish be angry, stupid?' Goss replies. 'They're just dumb creatures.'

'Didn't you see those dorsal fins on their backs, razor sharp, ready to cut us to pieces?'

'Wingfish?' exclaims Goss. 'That's all they are. They can't really harm us.'

'Anyway, the forest saved us, it stopped them from getting closer to us.' Hind looks relieved. 'The trees are on our side.'

'Yes, perhaps they are and maybe they'll help us to prevent Barco from getting back up the mountain. We must stop him.' Goss is emphatic. 'Otherwise, he'll tell the others about the Wingfish.'

'He is hindered now that he is carrying the girl,' says Hind.

'Yes, he was obviously enchanted by the fish girl.'

'You mean — you were.' Hind smirks.

'And are you sure it wasn't the Wingfish you fell in love with?' says Goss.

'No. There was something about that girl,' Hind says.

As if struck by lightning, Goss rises up, filled with a force of rage from head to foot. He lurches towards Hind. He punches him, catching him unawares and sending him reeling backwards, arms flailing, reaching out for the nearest tree. Before Hind can regain his balance, Goss pushes him against the trunk of a tree pushing his hands around his throat. He is screaming into Hind's face but his utterances are the guttural sounds that come from the belly; the bile rising with every vengeful thought he has ever held against his brother.

Hind begins to slip from Goss's hold, his whole weight is falling and for a split second Goss stops his attack. Has he squeezed the life out of him, has he killed his own brother? He halts for just long enough for Hind to recover his wits and raise his fist, but by now he is weak, too beaten to stand. But Goss does not give in and another punch angers Hind enough for him to be able to stand and fight back. They throw punches at each other's head and body, fall over branches, slamming into tree stumps. Their anger increases, subsumed in the terrible envy and hatred they have had for each other for all of their lives. Finally, they stop as abruptly as they began, and they are both lying on the ground, broken, noses bloodied, faces bruised, their clothing torn. The circle of glass is gone, it has slipped from Goss's pocket, into the undergrowth, squashed into the earth.

They are silent and then they begin to talk, in hushed voices at first, and it is as if nothing untoward happened, just like the passing of a storm that leaves behind a quiet devastation. The two of them lay on the ground, a single layer of dead leaves between them and the sticky floor. The night is getting darker, and the shadows deepening. The Ruba trees are dripping, silently, slowly. They ooze an odour that is unlike any other and it helps to send Goss and Hind into a deep sleep. Slowly, the forest embraces Goss and Hind, folding them in its sticky embrace.

19

'Omma, Omma,' Maysun calls into the semi-darkness.

Her voice is met with the silence of trees. The light is that of the filtering sky through the green leaves. She moves and cries out with the pain in her shoulder and folds her body back onto the ground. When the pain has eased, she opens her eyes, and rocking onto her good side she sits upright, all the time, restraining her cries.

She realises that she is inside the base of a tree because of the light that trickles in through the opening at the top; there are only leaves and branches between her and the sky. It must be an old tree to have grown so wide. In places, the bark is only a thin shell, a meagre protection from the forest. Unusually, it is not a Ruba tree, at least Maysun can see no hint of the sticky extrusions. She reaches out and touches the inner wall and it is damp, but not sticky — her hand comes away easily. Her eyes adjust to the gloominess.

She pulls at the thing that is heavy on her lap. It is the coat of an animal. As she pushes it away it has the smell of a creature she has never met, she is sure of that. The coarse hair catches in her finger nails and the texture is brittle. As it falls away, the pungent underside causes her to retch.

It is the garment that the boy was wearing, a jacket of skin and hair — the boy who tricked her with his strange dark eyes and who held out his hands as if he was welcoming her, as if he meant her no harm. And just as she felt herself believing, succumbing to his voice and his strange words, he tricked her. She touches her shoulder and feels the broken shaft of the arrow. She has been pierced from behind. The boy must have magic ways to be able to do that. But why would the boy hurt her, and why did he not kill her? Why would he bring her to this place in the forest? To hide her from others? Is she imprisoned? He might still be close by. Her whole body shakes as she tries to hold her breath, to listen, but there is no sound.

Perhaps he has gone to find food but he will not find it in the razed land of the valley and she will be left here to die, with no one knowing where she is. She thinks of her family, of her Pa, and then she begins to cry. Her sobs fill the hollow and echo until the sounds are great within her ears. She stops crying, and again, she listens. Perhaps he is hiding nearby, but she hears nothing, not even a snuffle of breath or a ruffle of leaves. She believes she is alone.

She touches her shoulder and knows what she must do. She feels along the shaft to where the arrowhead pierced her flesh. It moves slightly, sending pain through her, and she knows that it has not entered the bone. Then with one huge effort she clasps it tight and pulls and pulls until it is removed. Her cry of pain pierces the air.

Tentatively, she binds the wound with the plait of Gringrow from her pocket. She finds a dried but muddied mushroom in her pocket too and eats it, washing it down with water. With great sadness she recalls her Omma explaining how the mushroom was good for wound healing. Exhausted, she lays down and after a while falls into a feverish sleep interrupted only by the sounds of the night; a dripping filling the atmosphere as outside, the trees exude their night-time excretions, dropping their sap onto the forest floor.

Maysun is safe, deep inside the capsule of the tree. Her dreams are filled with creatures that she cannot quite see, they are just out of sight, and neither can she recognise their shapes. Contours, edges, shades, all shimmer in front of her, disappearing, re-appearing, whistling up from the depths of darkness, but when she looks at them directly, they disappear. Sometimes she rolls onto her injured arm and cries out in pain. Then she is awake and she sees only blackness but she feels the stealth of the air, and she is overcome with the odour of the animal skin until she again falls into a deep slumber.

She is dreaming that there is someone with her in the chamber. An elderly woman seated on the ground next to her is singing a lullaby, crooning and rubbing her hands, rolling her palms together as if warming a balm of wax. She wears a cloak wrapped tightly around her body, its hem spreading wide in an arc covering the entire floor of the inside of the tree. Maysun reaches out to touch the gown but she cannot feel it, and when she tries to touch it again, it melts under her fingers. But Maysun is unafraid. She comes to know that the old woman is the GrandOmma. And it is as if the woman can read her thoughts.

'Don't be afraid, my dear,' she says.

'Who are you?' Maysun asks.

'I think you know who I am,' the woman replies, 'but now, Maysun you must listen and you must trust me.'

'You know my name?'

'Of course,' the woman says, as if all this is normal. 'Your name is of the light of the moon, the beautiful face, the brightness that comes at the moment before the dark planet causes the Soomoon.'

Maysun takes a sharp intake of breath. She wonders why she was not told this before? She stares at the woman, blinking away her night tears. The woman says no more about her name.

'You must go to the Mountain,' she continues. 'You must climb and climb, all the way to the top until you find the cave with the stolen Wingfish.'

Maysun waits for her to carry on. She is barely able to look at the old woman whose cloak, even in the dark, has a brightness about it despite its dark green colour.

'How will I know which way to go?' Maysun asks.

'If you have doubts, then look for the pointed star and follow its direction. It will keep you on the path. But whatever happens, do not give up.'

Maysun turns away. She is not sure whether she is still dreaming or if she is imagining the cloaked woman. She closes her eyes and opens them quickly, turns back, to see if the phantom has disappeared. But she is still there.

'You will know the place when you have arrived,' GrandOmma says.

'But I cannot go through the Ruba woods, they are a place of great danger.'

'This is true but if you listen carefully, you will stay safe. The Wingfish are your friends and they will help you, as you must help them.'

'But they will not be able to come with me,' Maysun says, surprised. 'If they do, they will surely die.'

Maysun thinks about the Wingfish and how they can swoop up in ecstasy and reach so high, almost as high as the mountain, she believes, but she cannot believe that they could follow her up to the top of the mountain. For one thing, the Ruba trees would impede them. The thought of taking the Wingfish up the Mountain to their deaths upsets Maysun and she begins to cry again.

'All the Wingfish must be brought together,' GrandOmma looks at Maysun, firmly. She is adamant. 'They have been separated for too long from their kin and have been kept captive in the mountains for many years. It is time for them to return to the valley, and you are the Keeper of the Wingfish. It is your duty to bring them home.'

Maysun thinks about her Omma and the others of the Watterishi tribe. She wants to look for them, to bring them back together too.

'This is your mission, Maysun.'

'But how will I find them?' Maysun cries.

But it is too late. The GrandOmma, the apparition of the old woman has disappeared. The cloak has folded into the ground and become invisible. Only the dark soil of the inner tree is beneath Maysun now. The blackness of the hollowed tree has returned.

Maysun remains still, listening, waiting for a sign, something, anything, that will tell her that she is merely dreaming. She is sitting up, her eyes open, but there is nothing there, although she is sure that the GrandOmma really came to her and it was not just a dream. She leans against the wall of the tree and feels its gentle pulse against her skin and realises that the tree is listening, is alive.

She thinks about the Soomoon. She remembers how the ground began to move beneath her, how the great storm caused the earth to swell and ripple and quake, how the soil lifted into piles of mud and trees, and the rivers and lakes were drawn upwards to the sky. She has not seen her family, her friends, or any of the Watterishi since that terrible night — the night after she had whispered the word, and the world turned into a dark place. And just before the Soomoon came, the Wingfish who knew of its coming, were so frightened that they came to find her, Maysun, their only friend, the one who had betrayed their world. But they were beaten away, met by the women with the catch baskets and the men with their sticks.

20

Barco is sure that he can survive in the forest for as long as it takes to find the healing herbs, if only he searches during the daylight hours. He knows he must be vigilant while he looks for the rare plant whose leaves will prevent the wound of Maysun's shoulder becoming infected. And he knows that he need only turn his back for a few moments and he too may be attacked.

He still carries his bow and the quiver full of arrows on his back but they are of little use in the forest. Few rabbits or rodents survive here as the viscous floor of the Ruba forest is a trap for any who burrow or scavenge. The snakes are the survivors, with their cool sides they can glide over the mucilaginous bark, slowed down but hardly impeded by the Ruba. With their slow metabolisms, they hang for days and weeks in the same position without being imprisoned, the sticky sap of the Ruba being unable to adhere well to their slick bodies. They require little food, but they also provide little food to those who kill them.

It is late in the afternoon. Already, the threads of mucus are dripping from the trees. Barco is sure that he can hear voices. There is no one else in the forest, he thinks, apart from Goss and Hind. Surely, it cannot have been them who shot the arrow at Maysun, and escaped unseen, but even so, in his heart, he knows it must have been them. But perhaps someone else had acquired their arrows. They do not have the stealth or the quickness, and he cannot believe that they may have followed him without his knowing. But he can definitely hear voices. They are close by. Quickly, he drops to the ground and pulls himself up alongside a log, using it as cover. His breathing slows as he listens. Voices. Voices that are speaking in the tongue of the Watterishi.

'Come on, it can't be much further.'

Now, a different voice. 'But the trees are getting thicker.'

They are the voices of women, but they speak in a way that is more like singing than talking.

'Let's stop here,' one of them says.

'We need to find some dry branches to keep us from the floor.'

'Let's not worry about that. Come on, let's make a fire before it gets dark.'

He is surprised that he understands the meaning of what they are saying. He hears the differences, and he knows that they speak the language of the Watterishi, the same tongue as the girl by the lake. They are close by, so close that he can smell their perspiration. He knows that if he moves, they will hear him. He hopes they will go on, but they have stopped.

He is curious to see what they look like, and slowly, he lifts his head above the log. He sees one of them clearly, she is standing very close by with her back to him. She is wearing the same green garment as the girl by the lake; green, of a fibrous material. She has a long stick or spear in her hand which she is leaning on. These women must be the kith of the girl he has left in the tree. They are Watterishi, and now he knows that the girl was not the only one to survive the floods.

They have thrown their baskets onto the ground to begin the task of preparing for the night. One basket has tipped over and a loose log is rolling towards Barco, coming down, just about to pass his hiding place. Without thinking he puts out his foot. The log stops but his foot is sticking out and it could easily be seen by the woman standing close by. And if he retracts his leg, the further movement of the log will draw attention to him. In any case, it is too late. He looks up and sees a green dress, a green shawl, arms folded, the face of a woman, perhaps of a similar age to his mother when she died. She is standing in front of him, looking down.

Her hand goes to her mouth. She yells out. When the others hear her, they turn and run back.

Barco is sitting up now, his hands open in what he considers to be a gesture of peace. The other women begin to arrive; they carry sharpened sticks. One drops her basket on the ground and it rolls, like the small log, down the slope. Barco jumps to his feet, and runs but he does not get very far before he steps right into the basket, his foot becoming jammed in the bottom. He kicks out and tries to shake it off but the harder he kicks out the deeper the sharp edges of the reeds hold onto him. He falls to the ground. But before any of the women can reach him he is up again and running, his foot still in the basket. The reeds have drawn blood from his ankle and the faster he goes the sharper it stings. All around him he hears the echoes of their singing voices, ululating, penetrating the forest. He slows and then stops. He hunkers down, beside a large Ruba tree which is close to the stream hoping they will not see him. The sounds have become sharp and shrill. Soon they surround him.

'Please, please, I mean no harm,' he says, but they take no notice.

They cannot hear him above the noise of their own voices as they form a circle around him. There are at least six of them with their forked sticks and baskets and others on the outside of the circle are leaning in to look at him.

'I need help,' he says. 'It's for a girl, a Watterishi girl. A Watterishi.'

86

At the sound of the name of their tribe they stop. They repeat over and over: 'Watterishi, Watterishi, ishi, ishi...' He tries again to explain, but they cannot understand him but at least they are listening now and he tries to remember the words that he learned from the Peakerfolk elders. He speaks but the words are old-fashioned and clumsy, and soon they are laughing at him. At least they are not threatening him. So he repeats the words again and again and they laugh all the more. After a while they become quiet and talk among themselves; they watch as he dislodges his foot from the basket. They allow him to limp to the stream where he bathes his hurt foot. The women look as if they are trying to decide what to do with him but it seems that they cannot agree. Some are frowning and muttering, and others, their voices are rising in shrill leaps. Finally, they move closer to him again, pointing at him with their spear ends.

21

Goss pushes at the threads that are wrapping themselves around him, forcing them apart. He leans over towards Hind who is next to him on the ground. The white goo has already spread up Hind's legs, and the vine-like threads of Ruba are sprouting and pinning his arms to the ground. Other tendrils are working their way towards his neck. And just for a moment, Goss is fascinated. He watches the pulse on Hind's neck flickering and an artery growing bulbous. Hind seems to be fixed to the ground. He is motionless, asleep.

'Hind, get up!' Goss shouts, suddenly aware that he might be about to lose his brother. 'Now!'

Goss grabs and picks at the rubbery vines, pushing and shaking his bound sibling. Hind opens his eyes, raises his head a few inches. As soon as he sees the twine-like threads that have crept all around him he yells and tries to pull at the wefts of Ruba. But with each attempt he becomes more entangled and the more he struggles, the tighter he is tied. He is becoming infuriated, more and more incensed, and digging his fingers further into the tangle, struggling and pulling it away from his arms and body until he is able to sit up and is almost freed.

'That'll teach you,' Goss says.

Goss has recovered from his fright and he is laughing at Hind. Hind's face is reddening, becoming a purple, a bluish shade, until he still cannot speak. Some of the Ruba tendrils, having crept up his back and remained around his throat, are now closing around his neck. Gurgling sounds emerge from his mouth. Finally, Hind falls back onto the ground and starts to twitch. Goss leans over and as if slowly preparing for an operation he rubs his hands in a patch of dry soil. With swift movements he grabs the tendrils of Ruba from around Hind's neck and forces them apart, pulling and lifting the tangled threads into a bundle and flinging them into the bushes.

Hind is at once relieved and furious. He turns to face Goss who is now laughing at him, and with a deep, furious bellow, he shouts. 'I could have died!'

'Well you didn't, did you,' Goss states. 'So just mind where you fall asleep next time.'

Hind pulls himself up onto the log, rubbing his hands, his shoulders, his head and face. Then he carefully surveys the ground around him. He ignores his brother.

'Oh come on,' Goss says. 'Do you think I'd have let you die? My own brother?'

There is silence between them.

'Anyway, I'd have to explain to Jagg that my brother got scared of the trees.'

Hind thumps his fist down onto the log and turns to face Goss. But Goss quickly deflects his brother's ire.

'We'd better get moving,' he says, 'before the Ruba really gets us.'

Goss stamps at the fire that is still smouldering among the leaves and then kicks over the traces. He scatters the ashes and throws dry leaves all around until there is little evidence of a fire pit. Without further conversation, they stumble off into the forest making their way uphill to an area where the trees become thicker. Their limbs are sore, their bones ache, their hands and faces show the bruises and stains of their bloody fight and their tussle with the Ruba.

22

Throughout Maysun's childhood she was taught never to look towards the place where the peaks break the clouds with their summits. By doing so, the Watterishi believed that they would cause more rainfall, bringing down the sky-waters and drowning their homeland. Maysun dares not think about the events of the Soomoon but it is still very clear in her mind: the red moon rising, the fear of the Wingfish, the shock of seeing the grey ball of Ares in the sky, and the final evocation of the Soomoon.

She recalls the small details — her father tying the strong ropes around the sides of the hut, pulling them taut, and the way he called to Omma to come back inside. And how Omma refused.

'Leave the baskets!' he shouted. 'Let the Wingfish be.'

And she remembers the heat of the evening before the storm when the air was still and thick and filled with sounds of clicking fish.

She remembers her father telling her never to say the word, and when she could not help herself how she whispered, 'Soomoon, Soomoon,' and she looked up and saw the deepening glow of the red moon.

By now the grey dawn light has reached the edge of the forest and as Maysun falls in and out of fitful sleep, she dreams the same dreams over and over. She hears her father's voice but now it is fading as he repeats, 'Never say that word, never say the word,' but it is not really his voice, not the voice of the Pa she knows. And then there is a hand over her mouth as if it is trying to stop the word from coming out, and she is pushing it away, but it is only her own hand. And she knows it is too late to catch the word and put it back, it has already left her lips and been stolen away by the breeze. She cries out as she feels the pain of guilt, and shakes herself awake.

She pulls herself towards the entrance of the tree. The air is cold and she rubs her hands and stamps her feet. She reaches back in for the boy's jacket and pushes one arm into a sleeve, and tentatively rests the other side over the injured shoulder. She looks around her, one way and then the other, until she is sure she is alone and she steps out of the tree. Through the trees, some way below, she can see the lake and she knows that her journey up the mountain and through the forest has hardly begun. First she must return to the lake. As her feet press onto the soft floor she moves swiftly down towards the edge of the water.

The surface of the water is calm, at first, and then she notices the slightest swirl of the waters and then the little eruptions begin. Tiny pocks erupt followed by bubbles. The Wingfish are rising to the surface. Some are gliding to the edges, even grazing on the lingering Gringrows. She is glad for them. She bends down to lift the water into the bowl of her cupped hands and she washes her face and her neck. She fills the water pouch the boy has left her and gathers more Gringrow leaves for her journey. They will be enough to fill her belly and sustain her for many days.

The fish are aware of her movements, and they shiver as they near the edge as if they are waiting, listening out for the vibrations of her voice, but she will give no command, not today. She knows that they are safe where they are, and she will leave them for now. She tries to remember the face of the woman, the GrandOmma, who came to her in her dream. But just as it is with her father, she cannot recall her exact features, only the essence of the tone, the shape in the shadows. All that was once so familiar has changed, faded into a place of a previous time. Maysun knows she must be strong now; she is no longer the child, the daughter. She is the woman who has heard the voice of the GrandOmma. She has been privy to the tones of the great ancestor, and the beats of the rhythm are imprinted on the drums of her ears.

She looks up at the mountains. She sees their shape, their ridges, their peaks, the lines of snow. She tries to read them as if they might have a message for her but they are changing as she watches. Clouds are swirling around the peaks, puffing into an eternity of white sky, and elsewhere they descend, obscuring her view to where there is no horizon, as if the edge of the sky is nowhere, as if it is endless. She sees a rock, a sharp protrusion, above a sheer cliff, clean in the grey light and she knows that she must leave, to go on a journey through an impenetrable forest and climb the impossible mountain.

23

One woman is standing behind Barco, another has leapt over the stream and is blocking his retreat. Barco shakes his head but he is unable to move, the pain in his ankle is piercing even with the icy pressure of the stream water. They remain still, a tableau: the women with their spears, baskets scattered around the forest floor, Barco standing in the stream; the only movement comes from the water circling his ankles.

Barco knows that sooner or later they will move, one of them will say something, and then they will act. They will either kill him or take him as a prisoner, he has no way of knowing what they will do. The thought occurs to him that the Watterishi might have become cannibals in the intervening years since the wars with the Peakerfolk.

Then he realises that they are no longer looking at him, but they are looking all around as if checking that there is no more of his kind waiting in ambush. He thinks he has a chance but as soon as he moves, they all turn towards him. Slowly, he bends down and with his fingers he touches the water, lifting his hands to let the droplets fall. One of them beckons to him to come forward, but he continues with what he is doing. He scoops up handfuls of water and lets it splash back down. Another lets out a giggle, and very soon they all catch on and laugh out loud. He moves towards the bank and from the bare earth plucks and continues his movements with his hands and touching his mouth, as if he is reaping a luscious herb-filled ground. Then he makes the motions of gathering, armfuls of leaves and stems. The women are laughing all the more.

One woman, the one with a shawl of green fabric

wrapped around her head and shoulders, stares at him. She is the only one not laughing, and he sees that her eyes are a deep turquoise, shining bright even in this dim light. She signals to the others, waving her hand, and they lower their spears.

Two come forward and take hold of his arms and pull him out of the stream. With an arm around each shoulder they walk with him back to the place where he first saw them. There is a pile of sticks on the ground, and he sees that they have already started to gather tinder for a fire. He realises by the ashes scattered on the ground that this place has been used before and he wonders if the women have returned there or whether others have used this spot before them. He sits down where they leave him but they are watching him, waiting to see what he will do next.

He realises that he is no longer their prisoner and at first he thinks about running away into the forest but then he remembers his ankle. He turns it slowly one way and then the other. With relief he realises that it is not badly hurt, just a little sore, but it would be best not to run. Meanwhile, the women are clearing the ground and they do not seem to heed him. So he helps them to clear the ground and push stones into a circle to make a place for the fire. They gather dry leaves and fallen branches, some for the fire, and some to scatter over the sticky ground to make a barrier between them and the hungry soil. The women are tapping into the trees with hollowed out sticks. Barco wonders what they are doing; he has never seen this before. He watches as the Ruba juice slips through the hollow and into the collecting bowls that they have made out of the bark. He fears what they will do with this dangerous liquid but before long a bowl of Ruba juice is sitting on a tripod of long sticks above the fire, and another bowl is placed above it.

The woman with the turquoise-blue eyes is holding a sharp implement and looking at Barco. She is standing very close to him as she shows him the blade. He looks at it and with trepidation he nods in admiration. He sees that it is narrow and serrated, but most likely sharp enough to cut through a tough hide. Now she is pointing to her mouth, and he realises that she is indicating that she is hungry.

Suddenly she drops the knife. Blade point down, it slips easily into the forest floor. She looks at him then drops her eyes. Bending down and taking hold of the knife, the woman marks a circle on the ground, slicing through the soft soil. As she does this, a nub of a white fungus appears. She lifts out the fragile mushroom, then, she shows it to Barco. She makes out to bite into the fungus but first hands it to Barco. She still holds the knife in her hand and she is nodding at him. He bites into the soft flesh, she smiles, and he feels his tongue becoming clear, and as he swallows his hunger is sated; all with one mushroom.

Soon, more mushrooms have been collected, some are eaten raw, and others are cooked on the end of sticks over the fire. The bowl of Ruba juice has condensed and collected into the upper bowl and passed around for all to drink. Barco is aware that they are talking about him, they are speaking quickly and he can only understand a few of their words, but they are laughing. Perhaps it was his clowning in the stream that has amused them. In any case, he is not unhappy to be the butt of their joke. Better that, than at the butt end of a knife, or trapped in one of those baskets that look like the sharp-toothed jaws of a Wolfdog.

Eventually, the voices quieten and one by one they close their eyes and doze in the firelight. Barco's eyes are beginning to slip shut too. But he is aware of the woman with the turquoise eyes whose eyes remain open. Barco is dreaming of mushrooms, and he is distributing them from a great basket to all the Peakerfolk on the mountain. They are stuffing them into their mouths and laughing and laughing and patting him on the back. Then they are coughing, and their faces are changing colour. Their skin is turning from white, to blue, and then to indigo. He wakes with a start and finds that the light of the sun is piercing through the trees. It is hot, and it must be at least the middle of the day. He is alone. The women are no longer there. Perhaps it has all been a dream; perhaps he has been hallucinating.

But the fire was real. He is staring at the ashes, and he puts out his hand to feel the faint warmth. Next to him a black roach is crawling through the flakes of burned bark. The creature does not hesitate. No matter the size of the log, the weight of the stones at the edge of the fire pit, or the crumble or the heat of the ash; all is nudged to one side as it continues through the remains of the fire in a straight line as if nothing can deflect it from its course.

Barco sighs as he thinks about his mission; not only to save the Peakerfolk from starvation, but to find the herbs that will heal the wound inflicted by his kinsfolk on the Watterishi girl. As he stands up and looks around, he hears a cracking, a slight creak in the branches, and he wonders if the women are hiding in the trees and watching him, but he can see no one. The forest is deep and dark in all directions. He walks one way, looks and listens hard, and then he walks back the other way. He is sure that they have gone, and that he is alone. Almost sure. The cracking sound was so much like the pressure of a foot breaking a twig. He will hide at the edge of the camp for a while until he is sure that there is no one watching or waiting to follow him.

24

Maysun is slowly making her way through the trees. She has been climbing through the forest since the day began but she knows she is still not far from the lake, and now she is sweating profusely with the exertion and her injury. The ground is steep and she must pull herself from one tree to the next, resting only on the branches that are low enough and strong enough to hold her weight. She thinks about the boy whom she believes must have somehow shot the arrow at her, and is filled with fear. She sees him behind every tree and then when she looks again he has disappeared. She feels confusion too — his eyes, although strangely dark, held no malice, and she wonders why he wished to harm her. And if he wanted to destroy her, why did he take her into the woods, and then hide her inside a tree? Did he intend to come back and kill her? And then there was his jacket of coarse hair. Why did he leave it behind?

Meanwhile, the forest is becoming hotter with steam issuing from the undergrowth and she feels it in her throat, it is suffocating. But she must keep going, because if she does not she will sink down onto the Ruba floor. If she stops, she will be lost, entombed forever in the forest. The fear of this is enough to keep her going, but she is beginning to feel weary, she can see no end, no openings, no gaps. She has no way of knowing if she is going in the right direction or whether she is merely retracing her own steps.

The slope has levelled out and for a while it is easier, and soon the air becomes clearer as if the freshness of the mountains has pierced through the smog of the breathing trees. She is approaching a glade where the air is cooler, and she stops to rest by a rocky outcrop. From where she is sitting she can see sticks that have been burnt, their ends blackened like charcoal. There are dried leaves and stones but she knows that she is looking at the remains of a fire.

When she hears the snapping of a twig and a shuffling of leaves she drops to the ground and slowly she moves, crawling backwards to the edge of the glade, where the trees are thicker. Someone is there, they are coming, but who could dwell in this forest? Here there are signs of people; a fire built among the rocks.

The shuffling sounds comes from beyond the trees on the other side of the clearing. She keeps her head down; she is low, her body on the ground, head tucked under and she daren't look up. Directly in front of her, almost at the end of her nose, she sees something in the soil. It is shining, and she nudges it with her little finger. The soil that half covers it shifts easily. She remains flat on the ground as she lifts the object out. In front of her is a perfectly formed circle of glass. She can hardly breathe. Surely it cannot be? Not the same one? But there is only one like this, so Pa had told her.

It is her Omma's eyeglass, the one that has been passed on to her from her mother and her mother's mother and the mother before her. It was said that it came from the time of the first remembered Soomoon, when the eruptions caused by the nearing of Ares and the following meteorites sent shards of metal across the land. The eyeglass was formed from these celestial elements. She rubs it gently with her thumb, wipes away the soil from the markings at the edge. Yes. It is scored at the edges in the same way, in the same places as the one that belonged to her Omma. The familiar markings are inscribed in miniature in the lettering of the ancient Watterishi tongue.

Maysun looks out across the glade. How did the eyeglass get here? She cannot remember losing it, only that she picked it up at the place where she last saw her Pa. The vision of the mud almost makes her cry out but she tries not to think about it. Perhaps Omma is still alive, and she found the eyeglass and she has been sitting by the fire just a few hours before. If she hurries, she might catch her. Maysun rises, she is about to run across the open glade and into the trees, when she hears a rustle, this time it is coming from directly ahead. Someone is walking towards her. Again, she crouches onto the ground behind a small rock, and as she does, the eyeglass falls out of her hand, just out of reach, rolling along the open ground.

It is the boy, the one that was on the shore, the one who had been standing in front of her, the one who had her shot through the shoulder with an arrow. She touches her shoulder under the jacket sleeve. It is still very painful, and when she takes her hand away, there is blood. She is numbed with fear; she must escape before he sees her. She watches the boy as he kneels before the fireplace. He is lifting the leaves, looking at the ground; his expression is one of puzzlement. He stands up and looks all around, slowly turning to face the circle of trees. And now he is staring ahead, straight at the place where she hides. Maysun withdraws behind the rock but as she does her foot presses down onto a dry twig and it cracks.

Maysun remains still for what seems like a very long time, then she peers around the rock when she thinks it is safe but the boy is still there. He is looking at the trees on the other side now, studying the tops as they move in the breeze; he is looking one way and then the other. Finally, he nods as if he has made a decision, and he walks through a gap in the trees on the far side, and disappears from view. She waits a little longer until she is sure that he is gone and only then she slides herself along the ground, still keeping low, inching her fingers towards the eyeglass.

She takes hold of it and moves back to her former position, still hunched, looking out towards the shelter of the trees. She opens her hand and lifts the eyeglass up to her eye. She gulps in a breath as she is taken back to the lake; the lake of the Wingfish at the edge of the Ruba Forest. It is the same place where she was shot with the arrow. She takes the eyeglass out for a moment to make sure that she is not being watched, and then she replaces it. This time she can see the tree house where she had been left. But now, through the eyeglass, it is dusk, and already the trees are dripping with Ruba. She is inside the tree, and it is just how she left it.

It is as if she is there inside the tree, and she must find a way out. She sees a hand in front of her. It is beckoning her as if she is being invited, guided, drawn away from the tree. Now she is outside at the place where the lake is wide, and the sky is open. It is the old lake, the lake as it was before the storm, and she is standing on the beach, near the rocky promontory. She is calling to the Wingfish; her mouth moves around the words, 'Kiri Quar Kiri'. At that moment, it is not the fish that arise from the waters, but a single person. It is the boy. She gasps. The eyeglass falls from her eye.

She holds the eyeglass in the palm of her hand. She remembers Omma speaking to Pa about the eyeglass. 'It means nothing,' she said. 'It comes from the old times when the ancestors believed that the glass could tell the future, but no one believes in that now.' Maysun leans back against a tree, to maintain her balance and to keep herself from falling. She slips the eyeglass into the orbit of her eye, and once again, she is back at the lake, cautious, alert for any movement. When she is sure that she is alone, she climbs back onto the ridge and walks along to the end of the promontory that juts out into the lake. From here she can see that the water is thick and brown, and the blackened banks glisten in the light. All is quiet apart from the slow sucking, the plocks that come from the edges of the murky water. The surface of the lake is still, brown, and glassy.

'Kiri Quar Kiri,' she calls. She calls again and again, a little louder each time. She whistles the low breathy whoosh that is her secret way of calling the fish, of letting them know that it is her, and only her. But all is quiet, and she wonders if the fish are still there. Perhaps the eyeglass is showing her that the Wingfish have left, or worse; they have been poisoned by the murky waters.

The eyeglass steams over as her tears well and stream down her face. Life without the Wingfish is unimaginable. They have always been part of her life; they are her life, she is their protector. Then she remembers that if they sense danger, the Wingfish hide in the deepest cavities beneath the whirlpools; a place where no one dares to dive, where the motion of the water curls over deep caves in the basal rocks.

The eyeglass remains in place, in the socket of her eye, even as the tears are falling and flowing into the lake. She blinks, and first she does not see that the water is beginning to bubble and swell. Little humps appear in the water, at first they are like round-topped waves rocking and swaying as they come into the shore, but nothing breaks the surface. Perhaps the planet is shifting again. She looks again, harder, focussing on the lake. No, her feet are steady on the rock. The waters are rising.

With a spasm and a shake the waters part as the first Wingfish breaks the surface. It rises, twisting and turning in the sky. It is followed by another, and then another and the dozens are followed by the many as the surface of the lake breaks into life with the hops and leaps and splashes. Maysun holds her breath and then she shrieks in delight. They are flying through the air, all around her. The Wingfish tumble, gathering in a loop and speeding back and forth in the air, dipping and rising until they form a shape, a double loop. The sky is made entirely of the bodies of the Wingfish swirling around in a perfect sign of infinity. Maysun lifts one hand and the fish glide to her movements.

The eyeglass falls out of her eye. The world fragments, everything in front of her is becoming smaller, all the wisps of cloud, the slithering water, the soil and flesh of Wingfish are filtering back into the neck of a bell jar. And once again she is on the mountainside, deep in the Ruba Forest, and she is alone. The eyeglass is a mere slip of glass in her hand, reflecting the many shades of green from the trees. There are Ruba trees that go on for as far as she can see in every direction. She remembers the voice of the GrandOmma telling her to make her way up the Mountain to save the Wingfish. She knows what she must do. She must find the mountain where the Wingfish are imprisoned.

She looks at the eyeglass in her hand. If only it would not just let her see, but help her. At that moment the trees begin to shake and then the branches rattle. She is startled and scared. From behind her, from all around, from deep within the forest comes a rush of wind, a whistling, and a flapping. The sky darkens above her, a swarm of creatures fill the sky, and then she sees them; the Wingfish are here, all around her. They have found her in the forest; she has drawn them to her through the eyeglass.

They come towards her, low down, almost touching the ground. They are fizzing and swarming until she can hardly breathe. She fears they cannot survive so far from the lake and she waves her arms to send them back to where they are meant to be, but they continue to buzz and flutter around her. She sings and shouts out her commands. How will they survive without the waters of the lake? But they no longer follow her instructions. They have come very close to her, they are touching her, jabbing at her with their open mouths, and for a moment, she is afraid. And then she realises that she is no longer standing on the ground, she is above it, rising high into the trees.

The Wingfish are lifting her, their bodies flapping and pulsing, and coaxing her upwards, higher and higher, until she is above the canopy of the forest. She looks down and she can only see the tops of the trees. Then gently, they drop her onto the largest, leafiest bough. Maysun grasps hold of a branch and as it sways she looks down at the ground far, far below.

25

Barco has not been in the forest long enough to know the source of every movement, but he was sure that he heard something in the trees on the other side of the clearing. He walks towards it, at first checking the fireplace but the only signs are of the women and the trail they have left. From that he sees that they are making their way back down the mountain. Perhaps they have decided that they are better to go back to the valley now that the storms have finished.

He leaves the glade and finds a trail that meanders one way and then the other until it comes to the stream where the skirmish of the previous evening happened. He is still surprised that he missed the departure of the women, and that they left so quietly without him noticing. The forest is clear in the daylight and it is easier to negotiate his way. Barco is watchful, looking out for rivulets where the herbs are most likely to grow. He collects the milfoil leaves by the stream and hunts for the tiny blue flowers that will prevent the arrow wound becoming infected but there are none to be found.

He walks along; his way is made easier by the breeze that has sprung up and is coming from behind him. It is unusual to feel the wind in the deepest places of the forest but it does not last for long. He thinks about the woman with the turquoise eyes, the one who had spent the night sitting by the fire, fighting off the need to sleep. There was something about her that haunted him. The women were of the same kind as the girl, and probably same tribe of Watterishi, but he had been unable to tell them about the girl or ask them if they knew her.

He is coming to another clearing, but this time there is

a single tree standing in the centre. It is not a Ruba tree but one that has a broad bulbous trunk. He wonders if he has inadvertently retraced his steps and walked full circle, and now he has come across the tree with the chamber where he left the girl. Slowly, he edges around the clearing and works his way around to the back of the tree. He sniffs. There is a familiar scent in the air; a leathery, acrid smell.

He had forgotten all about Goss and Hind, but now he recognises their taint in the air. When he is within three leaps of the tree, he hears the sounds of breathing, the intake, the out breath, louder than most; it is the sound of snoring, and for a moment he is relieved. At least, if it is Goss and Hind, he knows them well enough that if they are asleep they will not easily awake. He listens intently as the breaths double and falter and snort.

Near the entrance he sees two pairs of feet. They are poking out from the base of the tree. Across each pair of shins the hem of a Stonebear jacket and on the feet are the hide boots of the Peakerfolk. Barco moves quietly around the back of the tree. A low branch is within reach, and he pulls himself up onto it. His plan is to draw the pair out and get them away from the girl, Maysun, if indeed she is there, and if it is the same tree. The creaking of bark on bark momentarily halts the breathing of the pair on the other side but it soon resumes.

Barco climbs up to the mid-way branches, pulls himself up and sits in the fork of a branch. He pulls the larger leaves around him to act as a camouflage. He is not sure what his plan is, only that he wishes to remain hidden should Goss and Hind awake. While he is wondering what to do next, he finds a stone in his pocket. He rolls it around his hand, then he throws it into the air and catches it. He throws it again, but this time he misses it. It falls and rumbles from one branch to another until it hits the ground on the other side, only it is not the ground that it hits. The stone has landed on the foot of a slumberer. It sends a jolt up through the tree as its owner jerks awake.

'Hey, what was that for?' Hind exclaims.

For a moment Barco thinks that Hind is talking to him until he remembers that he cannot be seen. He waits for Goss to reply.

'What're you on about?' Goss demands. His voice echoes from inside the tree.

'The stone, you idiot.' Hind says, pointing at the ground. 'You threw a stone at me.'

'What are you on about?' Goss repeats rubbing his eyes, having crawled forward to peer out of the tree.

'Look!' Hind holds up the round stone close to Goss's face.

'Yes, it's a stone.' Goss sighs. 'Clever you.'

'But if you didn't throw it, where's it from? It's all mud around here. No rocks.'

'How can a stone land on me,' insists Hind, 'if it hasn't been thrown?'

'How do I know?' Goss replies. 'I was asleep, dumbhead!'

Hind won't be drawn into another fight. He is looking all around as he gets up and begins to walk around the tree.

As he returns to the opening Goss says with a snigger. 'Maybe it's the ghost of the girl.'

Barco listens carefully.

'Don't be stupid,' Hind replies. 'Anyway, the girl was by the lake right down in the valley. Her ghost wouldn't come all the way up here.' His voice is shaky now. 'And, we don't believe in ghosts.'

'Don't we?' Goss replies, lazily.

'It's just you and me here.' Hind's voice lowers, almost to a whisper. 'Isn't that so?'

'That's for sure.' Goss is still comfortable in the warm interior of the tree. 'But maybe there's a snake.'

'Snakes!' says Hind, agitated.

Barco's foot slips, only slightly, but Hind sees it as a slithering movement. 'Yes! They're in the tree.'

'Snakes! Where?' Now Goss is on his feet. 'Let's get out of here, quick!'

Barco has shut his eyes and he is holding his breath. The tears are running down his cheeks as he watches Goss and Hind running off into the forest, pulling up their trousers as they go, leaping and skipping over the ground. Then, when they are out of sight, he bursts with laughter. Barco leaps down from the branches, pulls off the leaves from his body. He checks inside the tree. It is empty and he is sure that it is a different tree from the one where he left Maysun.

He knows where Goss and Hind are now and he knows in which direction they are headed. He will keep a little way behind them but near enough to be sure of where they are. At least now, he knows that the girl is safe from Goss and Hind, and that they are heading back up the mountain. Maysun's kinswomen will most likely find her on their return and they will look after her. But Barco knows how difficult it can be to remove an arrowhead, and he still intends to find the healing herbs and return.

26

All is silent. The Wingfish have disappeared and all that is left are the tiny droplets from their fins lingering in the air. Maysun is holding onto a branch. She daren't look down, but soon she realises that the canopy is so dense, so impenetrable, that she cannot fall, not even if she were to try. She crawls along to where the branches grow close together, criss-crossing each other, and she lies down facing the enormous sky. The tree tops are fresh and green without the sticky extrusions of the Ruba at a lower level. She relaxes, almost forgetting her fear, and just for a moment she is floating on top of the world, held aloft by a carpet of leaves.

The light is fading and she is ready. Carefully, rising and stepping forward, and keeping her arms outstretched to keep her balance she tentatively steps out, one foot in front of the other, all the while looking out for holes, gaps in the leaves and cracks through which she might see the forest floor — but there are none. Before nightfall, she has made her way further and further up the mountain, walking on the topmost branches and leaves, the rooftop of the forest. The distance she covers is greater than if she had traversed through the forest at ground level.

Her way ahead is clear, just a sea of leaves below an empty sky, and when she looks back so too is the way behind. In fact, whichever way she looks, upwards, downwards, to either side: she is surrounded by the waving tops of the Ruba trees. She stops to rest. She takes out the water pouch that the boy had left for her in the tree chamber and she drinks, swallowing deeply, and then she chews at the Gringrows. As she reaches into her pocket her fingers touch the cool edge of the eyeglass but she does not take it out. Soon she is relaxed, lying down on the leafy branches and falling asleep, but she remains in a light sleep, waking momentarily to grasp the branches around her, although it is apparent that she is in no immediate danger.

It is deep in the night when Maysun hears a voice. She looks around her but the night is too dark to see, there is only one clear star in the sky, the one with the spikes of light coming out of it, the one spoken about by the GrandOmma. The Moon has almost disappeared, casting a shallow light.

Maysun hears a rustling in the leaves. Surely no other creature could climb to this height, but there is no doubt that the leaves are moving, swaying in a slight breeze. It is as if there is someone approaching.

'Loa,' Maysun whispers. Her voice is shaky. 'Loa,' she repeats. This time louder.

Nothing. But something is rising and emerging through an opening in the canopy. She repeats the greeting over and over until she is crying out her salutation in fear. The thing is next to her and she feels its warmth, and a folding around her shoulders. Could it be an arm, a wing, a cloak? Still she can see nothing.

'Loa, Maysun,' a voice comes from within the trees. 'Have no fear. You will not fall.'

'Who is this?' Maysun asks. 'GrandOmma, is that you?'

Maysun can feel the breath issuing from the mouth with a softness and a gentle lilt of its voice.

'I have come to you with a warning.' It is the voice of the GrandOmma. 'Never look for the answer in the eyeglass.'

'I do not understand,' Maysun says. It is true that only a few moments before Maysun had been dreaming about the eyeglass.

'The eyeglass will reflect your anxieties, everything you have witnessed in the past, and all you fear for the future,' the gentle voice continues. 'But it is only by your strength, the strength you carry within you, that your mission will succeed.'

The words are followed by silence, the deep soundlessness of the night; neither cry of beasts, nor flight of birds or flutter of Wingfish. Maysun waits for GrandOmma to continue but the warm breath is replaced by the sharp air of night.

'Loa, Loa,' she calls, 'are you still there?'

There is no reply and soon Maysun sinks back into the leafy layers and falls asleep.

She wakes as the light of a new day is unfolding, as the first mists leave the cover of the forest. When she sits up she is frightened that she will fall but then, slowly, she stands, stretches her arms up and out and checks the balance of her body. When she is ready she continues to tread her way across the rooftop of the forest, up and up the mountain.

27

All night long the howling of the Wolfdogs is ceaseless. Sometimes they are faint calls that end with a muffle, a smothering, as if from the closing of the trees, at other times the calls are sharp, piercing. At each crescendo, Worro tilts his head to one side, then raises it up and howls. He stays by the door, and when Dorca calls him to come over to the bed it makes no difference; he seems captivated by the calls. With every rise, every wail, he scratches at the door, sniffing at the base, and then he howls and barks a response.

Dorca and Carew are disturbed when they hear shuffling. It seems to be directly outside, so close that they believe there must be a creature nuzzling at the door, prodding and pushing to find a way in. There are thuds, followed by yelps, and then silence. As the door quivers and shakes Dorca and Carew look at each other nervously. Worro cowers.

'Perhaps you should go and find out what it is?' Dorca says.

But Carew shakes his head.

'Best leave well alone,' he says. 'We don't want any trouble.'

Even in the dark Dorca can see the glint of fear in his eyes.

All is as silent as the night is black. It is as if all the Wolfdogs have been swallowed, gulped into a black vortex. Worro has slipped under Dorca's bed but his ears twitch and now and again his paws drag at the floor. Finally, he gasps and his great sighs vibrate throughout the cave.

Dorca is the first to waken. The morning light is grey, a kind of dead grey that feels as if all life has been sucked away by the night and the new day is struggling to be born. A hush has fallen over the mountain world; no air moves as if all of life is contained in a frozen moment. Dorca shivers and then she notices the door at the cave's entrance is open. She sits up. Through the opening she sees a trail of blood, bright, almost fluorescent on the fresh snow.

'Carew, Carew, wake up.' Her voice is brittle. But Carew is sleeping now and is slow to emerge from his bearskin.

'Worro?' Dorca calls. 'Worro?'

Carew hears the panic in Dorca's voice and rises quickly. Worro the Wolfdog is gone.

'He must have gone to look for Barco,' he says.

'Look at the blood,' Dorca says. 'We must go after him.'

'No Dorca. That would be crazy. It is not safe.'

'We can't just leave him.' She is becoming distraught. 'We made a promise to Barco.'

'He'll not find Barco,' Carew says slowly, 'and then he'll come back.'

'You don't know that.' Dorca is flushed. She is angry with her father. 'Worro may be lying hurt somewhere, he might have been attacked. He will not give up until he finds Barco. I know.'

'We can't expect him to understand...'

'...I know what you're saying. How can a mere Wolfdog understand? But still...'

28

Maysun can feel the freeze in the air. The chill is greater than anything she has felt before, as if an ice cold blade is pressing against her body. She shivers but at the same time sweat from her head is obscuring her vision. She feels for the wound on her shoulder. The Gringrow plait has soaked up much of the blood, and she believes her wound is healing.

She can see the end of the forest now. As she reaches the final rows of trees she is surprised to find that here they finish abruptly, in a straight line, not, as she imagined, a petering out, growing less and less dense. The trees remain as close and upright up until the last – and then there is the ground, a long way below.

Even the canopy remains interwoven and compact until the final tree, and it is difficult to reach the main branches below. She sees an opening but with her first attempt her foot slides off a branch and she falls. She catches hold of a branch and dangles dangerously. She leans to one side but she must pull herself up unless she is to fall. As she looks down she can see the forest floor, lit by the light of the Marginlands. It is a long way down. She is shaking and her arms and hands are weakening. As she clings to the branch her injured shoulder seers with pain. Her ears are filling with a swishing like the throb of blood. She fears that at any moment she will slip away with fear or into unconsciousness. She can hold on no longer and as the pounding increases, there is a sensation along her legs, her body, her face, and a rush of wind as she falls from the branch.

'Omma, Omma,' she calls.

She braces herself and believes she will soon hit the

forest floor, and she will be no more. And just as it happened before, she hears a mighty whoosh and she gulps as her breath is snatched away. But she has not fallen very far, she can still see the forest floor a long way below. And now she is surrounded by the bodies of the Wingfish who buffer and lift her high above the trees and over the edge of the forest. She is falling again, but gently this time, as if floating, swaying from side to side towards the ground like the falling of a leaf.

The whispering has stopped and she is on the ground, barely able to stand. But she cannot stop and feel thankful for even a moment. Those soft sounds made by the Wingfish have been replaced by the grinding and a gnashing of jaws. In front of her are rows of teeth, incisors framed by long canines, sharp enough to tear her apart, and saliva dripping from the hungry lips of yellow-eyed beasts. These must be the creatures of the mountains that she heard tales of from the old storytellers — stories of the evil Wolfdogs who wear the skins of other animals, who live within the rocks and breathe fire into the night.

The Wingfish are still with her, quivering, surrounding her as if they are trying to protect her, flying to and fro, zipping away from the jaws that snap at them. But the Wingfish are weakening, they no longer have the strength to lift her, all their energy has been used to reach the edge of the forest from the nearby stream and they need to return to it as soon as they can. They had followed Maysun by way of the stream, leaping from pool to pool, while she traversed the canopy.

Now these monsters of hair and teeth snap at the Wingfish. Some catch hold of them and run off with their prey, others tear at the gills and wings until many of the Wingfish have fallen to the ground, their bloodied guts strewn around them. They are quickly eaten. Then the evil creatures return to the girl, forming a circle around her; their eyes are yellow and glowering, they are snapping and snarling, baring their teeth. Maysun crouches down as far as she can, her arms over her head. She pulls the boy's jacket closer around her as she fears they will catch the scent of her wound and tear her apart. She is crying, her head buried in her hands. They are about to leap towards her.

She opens her fingers just wide enough to see the ground a little way in front. A trail of saliva, above four giant paws, is twisting in the air. Finally, she looks up. A single Wolfdog has come forward — he is the largest of the pack. The others move back and allow him to circle around Maysun. He comes in close, almost touching her, sniffing at the jacket. Perhaps he wants her all to himself, to rip her apart and devour her just as the others have done to the Wingfish. She shudders. Her slight movement sends waves that ripple across the pack.

The leader Wolfdog stands in front of Maysun, he rises onto his back legs at full stretch, his claws like daggers. Maysun cries out. The Wolfdog's chest expands as he inhales and as he lifts his head a flash of the moon catches his teeth, and he lets loose a howl that echoes around the mountains. The other Wolfdogs yap and snap and pounce forward, nipping into the centre of the circle as if they are about to challenge their leader. One even bounds towards him but the giant Wolfdog lunges, drawing blood from the neck of the upstart until the younger Wolfdog retreats yelping. The others cease their din, they turn away and run into the dark of the mountain. The large Wolfdog turns too and with one last look at Maysun he disappears after the pack.

29

Carew has made two bowls of porridge from the remnants at the bottom of the grain sack. It will be enough to keep them going for a day.

'Worro!' Dorca calls out as the Wolfdog appears. He limps as he enters the cave but he makes his way to Dorca and licks her hand. His ears are down as he slumps to the floor, head between his paws.

'The poor thing must be exhausted, he's been out all night,' Dorca says. 'Poor Worro, poor Worro,' she croons, but the Wolfhound only glances up at her for a moment before burying his head in his paws. His coat is coarse and knotted, matted with sprigs and bits of grit as if he has been dragged through the wildest of places.

Dorca looks shocked as she pulls a twig from his coat. 'I believe he must have been to Theravada,' she says. 'Look at these tiny seed heads. See how they are close to the stem. They are the ones that only grow on the high ranges.'

When a Wolfdog dies, whether from natural causes or old age, the others gather at night at a special place in the mountains. Known to the Peakerfolk as Theravada, it is a place beyond the tracks high up in a cleft within the ranges to the east, beyond the Mountains of Qar, and only visited by the few who dare. The Wolfdogs trek for many hours, scavenging all they can find on the way. Even the best Wolfdog will follow his instinct in the end, even one as well trained as Worro, who has lived with the Peakerfolk since puppyhood.

Worro snaffles the grainy porridge that Carew puts in front of him and then begs for more.

'That's all, Worro, there's no more,' Carew says.

Dorca is picking out the sticky seed heads and prickles that have snagged in Worro's coat. But he cannot keep still, he is far too restless and he begins to bark and then to growl. Someone is knocking at the door. Worro bares his teeth.

'It's early for a visitor,' Carew says. 'Who can this be?'

He pulls open the wooden door to their cave-home. A girl is standing in the doorway. She is huddled inside a huge coat, her mother's perhaps, judging by how it touches the ground, and the arms fall way below her fingertips. Worro is at the entrance and he looks at the child, his head to one side and then to the other. He begins barking but the girl remains perfectly still, unafraid, it seems.

'It's all right, Worro,' Dorca calls. 'Shush!'

'Welcome, Sali. Come in,' Carew beckons her inside. 'Come out of the cold.'

The girl enters. She is the daughter of a neighbour, the youngest of a family of five. Her small pale face protrudes from the hood of the great coat. She looks hungry and gaunt. Carew puts a hand on the child's shoulder and steers her towards the table where he offers her the scrapings of the porridge from his own bowl. While Sali slurps and licks the bowl clean, Worro goes over to her. He sniffs at her clothes and lets out a whine.

'Worro,' Dorca calls. 'Leave her alone.'

'He'll be smelling the smoke from the Wolfdog meat,' Sali says.

Both Carew and Dorca looked shocked. 'What do you mean?' they ask in unison.

'Last night,' the girl says, 'they captured one of the wild Wolfdogs, it was an old one, really old, it wouldn't have lasted long...'

'They killed a Wolfdog and ate it?'

'Yes,' the girl says, her eyes are wide open. Her cheeks are marked by a trail of tears and dirt.

'So that explains where Worro must have been,' Carew says looking at Dorca.

The young girl, Sali shrugs her shoulders.

30

'Hang on,' Hind shouts. 'Not so fast.' He is out of breath, panting, unable to keep up with Goss, who is zigzagging his way up the hill, lifting his feet higher as he runs.

Eventually, even Goss cannot continue and he slumps to the ground but leaps up when he remembers how the fibrous tentacles of the sticky Ruba tried to trap him before. Goss and Hind have come to the remains of a large fallen tree, one that has rotted and covered the ground with its speckled remains. They fall onto the clean root nubs that stand proud of the earth.

After a moment when they have caught their breath, Goss points towards a close-knit group of trees below them.

'Do you see what I see?' Goss whispers.

'Do I see what?' Hind asks.

'There's someone down there, I'm sure of it. Look!' Goss is pointing to the area of trees they have recently circumnavigated — an area of dense Ruba where the boughs are low to the ground. They watch as the branches spring back as if they have been recently disturbed.

'There's no wind,' Goss says. 'It would take a bear to move a branch like that.'

'A bear?' Hind's voice is shaky.

'Or a person.'

It is then that they both see the jacket-less form of Barco, his back with its slung bow and quiver disappearing out of sight.

'Barco,' Goss says slowly, quietly. He squeezes Hind's arm and puts one hand over his mouth to stop him from speaking.

They watch Barco heading crossways through the

forest. He is still a little way behind them. Goss beckons Hind to follow. First they slip around the back of the tree, peer around the side, and when they are sure the way is clear, they move on to the next tree, swiftly, watching out all the time. Before long, the ground is becoming loose, full of shale. They stop.

'This is what we will do.' Goss whispers his plan into Hind's ear.

They go back to where the ground is firm and work quickly and quietly, dragging sticks along until they have made several shallow gullies. Then they collect the dry tinder and dead branches, breaking them into smaller pieces and placing them along the gullies. All the time they are looking out for Barco, but there is no sign of him. Finally, Goss pulls the flint stone and knife from his pocket and strikes the two together until sparks fly, and he can light the bunch of dried leaves held in the hands of Hind. The leaves smoulder, then smoke, then tiny sparks fizzle, and as they do, Hind places them onto the ground among the twigs.

The fire merely smoulders at first but then it flickers and runs along as if chasing a rodent into a tunnel, tinder catching tinder. Soon the larger dead branches catch, and the fallen Ruba beans bubble and spark, and soon the fire burns. They repeat this along each depression and when all are alight, they cover them, lightly kicking loose soil over the channels of fire. Now the earth is oozing grey smoke, like clouds trapped in a mist. The effect is a wall of smoke.

'That should do it,' Goss said. 'He will never find his way now.'

They hug and for one moment they are brothers again, bonded by their wickedness. They laugh as they watch the smoke wafting into the air, circling and puffing.

31

The wolf creatures have gone. Maysun stands up and looks back at the forest, then to the mountains rising in front of her, and along the ridges to the west and the east. There is nothing else here. She is alone.

'Kiri, Quar, Kiri,' she calls quietly at first, hardly more than a whisper. Then again, louder. No Wingfish appear.

The Wingfish have flown away, frightened off by the Wolfdogs. At least not all have perished in the attack, she thinks, but she worries that those who escaped will soon be in need of water and she hopes they will make it safely back, dipping into the streams that course down the mountain on their way to the valleys of the Watterishi. Before she leaves, she holds her hands out, open to the sky, and she sings a wordless song, her voice ululating, spiralling upwards.

She sets off along the edge of the trees until she comes to a stream. The water rushes and bubbles around, seeping into the soil, and her feet soon become sodden. Where the stream meets the beginning of the forest the plants are abundant but she does not recognise them. They do not have the curled foliage of the lake but they look to be most succulent and some are crisp and white. She drinks from the stream and then she picks one of the juiciest leaves and nibbles at it. It is both sweet and bitter and once she has tasted one she wants more. There is only one patch of these protruding through the stony bank, and she is careful to leave a few in order that they may continue to flourish. The plants are not as tasty as the Gringrows but they fill her empty belly and the cold water feels smooth on her sore throat as she swallows.

She pushes a few more leaves into her pouch and she

walks on. After a while the path disappears — the ground is broken up by the scree of a shale ridge. Ahead of her are the higher slopes of the mountain with their white glistening tops, the ones she has often seen from the valley. The wind is stronger the higher she goes and it bellows in fits and starts and the sudden gusts startle her. She slips several times, sliding back down the mountain before she can ascend again. Her ears are filled with the noise of the wind and at times she thinks she hears the buzz of the Wingfish, and she smiles and looks around expectantly, but there is nothing there. Everything below her is barren and dark.

The ground is harder, crunchy under foot, and she realises that she has now stepped onto the crystal white carpet that lays between the rocks. She has often wondered at its beauty from below when the sunlight on the white mountain pierces the sky, and at other times, how the shadows of the clouds produce a million shades of white and grey as they pass over. And how the white patches change shape, increasing and decreasing, shifting according to the season. Now she is no longer curious; she feels only the bitter cold, and she is afraid.

She pushes her cold hands into the pockets of the jacket and she touches the tip of the eyeglass and she is comforted by its smoothness. Perhaps Pa was right, the glass lets you see into places and times that do not yet exist but the GrandOmma has sowed doubt in her mind. She would like to be comforted — she would like to look into the glass and see Pa and Omma back in the stilted house, Omma cooking the Gringrows and Pa in his rocking chair giving advice to anyone who will listen. She smiles at the thought but she knows in her heart that it is all gone — the huts, the village, the boats. They no longer exist, all has been washed away with the Soomoon, every single stick sucked into the mud. Many of her friends will be gone too, washed away and drowned. She wonders if some have survived and that one day they will be reunited. She dares not to think about Omma but she will not give up hope. She is determined that she will return with the Wingfish and reunite them with their brethren, and bring calm and peace to the valley. She hopes that the swelling of the Red Moon and the black ball of Ares will never collude against them again. But for now, she will leave the eyeglass in her pocket.

She has found a track to follow and the path has become easier. But she sees locks of coarse hair lying amongst the stones and foul faeces that darken the rocks and she realises that the path might not be safe — she may be following the trail of the Wolfdogs. Her feet are hurting in their flat woven shoes that are made for the soft mud shores of the valleys. They are fragile on the sharp scree. Blisters are forming on her feet but she dares not stop to tend to them. She only hopes that if her feet bleed they will not leave a trail for the Wolfdogs to follow.

She has almost reached the higher rocks before the peaks begin when she sees a shallow opening ahead of her, possibly a cavern or perhaps it is a natural scoop in the cliffs. As she comes closer she sees that it is set deep enough for her to be able to shelter from the wind. Here the ground is darker, flecked with charcoal. She thinks she can smell the faint taint of smoke in the air but perhaps, after all, it is an old fireplace judging by the scattering of small bones that show no sign of charring but look as if they have been whitened by the motion of the winds or bleached in the stark mountain light.

Maysun ponders on these thoughts when a shadow falls across the hollow. She cannot see anything at first but her instinct is to hide and she backs into the rock. She can see enough to know that the creature is standing upright and from the head it seems as if wild snakes are sprouting from it and twisting in the breeze. The creature is moving towards the fire pit. But this is no wild animal but the silhouette of a man. He wears the coats of animals and his hands hang at his sides, large and rough. He is as tall as a five-yearling tree and has a beard that reaches to his knees. She cannot see his face now above the beard — it is covered with a matting of leaves or moss and when he turns she sees that his eyes are bright in the dimming light.

'Loa,' Maysun calls. 'Loa.' Perhaps he will know where the Wingfish are kept, she thinks.

But he does not reply. He is moving away and beckoning for her to follow. Cautiously, she follows making sure that she leaves enough distance so she can run and escape. She glances down to the dark trees in the valley and for a moment considers rushing past him through the scree and down the mountainside.

The man moves slowly, lumbering, and she sees that he is very old and that she could easily outrun him. Now he is beckoning and pointing, indicating that she should follow the path that goes around the side of the rock. He points to a gap under a ledge. She looks at it and realises that it is the entrance to a cave. Is this his home? Does he want her to go inside?

She is fearful for a moment and looks behind her to make sure she knows the path. When she looks back at the stranger, he has gone. He is nowhere to be seen, as though he has simply disappeared. She walks to the entrance of the cave, again looking behind her and all around but she sees nothing, no one. She enters the cave and to her surprise, it is filled with light, a filtered light that comes from the gaps in the roof, tiny openings bordered by the thin vegetation. Drops of icy water drip onto her head. She shivers.

Ahead of her, the cave splits into two passages, one to the right and one to the left. She closes her eyes tightly, as if to seek out the right way with her intuition, and she feels drawn to the passage on the right. She touches the wall in a need to steady herself, and she looks back towards the entrance. The light has faded but the entrance to the cave is suddenly illuminated by a flash of lightning. She turns back and sees that the passageway ahead is almost completely dark but she has seen enough that she can continue. There is a rumbling. A storm is breaking, but it continues on, a regular roar, a grumbling like a persistent snorer, as if there might be a creature sleeping within the mountain. The rumbles gather until she feels a draught blowing over her, pushing her forward. She can hardly breathe with the swiftness of the air rushing from behind her and past her. Then, as quickly as it has arrived, it is gone, and the air returns to the chilled stillness of the outer cavern, and the odour of damp that exists in all the dark places.

32

Barco rubs his eyes. They are stinging, and his legs and body feel tired from climbing through the forest. He has followed Goss and Hind but he has lost their tracks as the mists arise in swirling currents, billowing and puffing around him. The heat rises rapidly, an unusual increase that has taken him by surprise, and the steam affects his vision, his sight blurred, his eyes watering. He soon realises that it is not steam but that it is smoke. He coughs, just a little at first but then when he can hardly catch his breath he begins to panic. It seems he cannot inhale, not fully, and he can only take in shallow breaths. His throat is constricting and he clasps his hands to his chest and his neck.

He sees an orange glow flickering among the trees, a glow that at first he had thought was the light from the rising sun. Flames are leaping from tree to tree, smoke is engulfing the forest in front of him, and little flames are chasing a line in the ground. He stamps on them, but as each flame is quenched, more appear, leaping towards him. He turns around and sees that behind him all is as it was, the familiar dark and damp of the forest, the dripping trees are ignorant of the approaching fireball.

Ahead of him the trees are alight, their tinder bark easily sparked by the spitting Ruba. There is one almighty crack followed by an explosion as a tree comes down crashing through its neighbours shedding sparks and blocking the path. The fallen tree continues to burn and the oily substance of the Ruba begins bubbling and oozing until the forest floor is slick with the loosening rubbery tendrils.

Barco shields his face and ties his neck scarf around

his mouth. He is sweating and as he rubs his arms he feels the hairs that are singed falling away. He has almost reached the upper edge of the forest and he knows that if he can make his way a little further along he will come to a cutting through the trees where a stream has previously forged its way into the forest from the Mountain. He knows it well. During the winter months, it becomes so swollen with snowmelt that even the great Ruba trees cannot halt its course.

There is a temporary lull in the billowing smoke and he sees the mountain of Qar ahead. He knows that as long as he follows this direction he will come to the edge of the forest where the stream enters. He must run before it is too late. He sees a gap where the fire has already razed and blackened the ground. He ties the scarf firmly around his head and moves as quickly and as lightly as he can, barely touching the ground. Soon the ground is becoming softer, which means that the old stream cannot be far. He also knows its dangers, that he risks being sucked into the deep liquid soil of the forest floor around the stream, and with each step the ground pulls at his feet. He can see the edge now and the gap is ahead, in the distance, but on either side there are trees flaming and firing and threatening to fall around him. He lurches forward.

There is a great shudder and a crack that shocks him seconds before the crash of an ancient tree. Barco freezes not knowing for sure which direction the tree will go but this time he is safe; the tree has fallen the other way. From his position on the ground he sees that, to the left of him, there are figures moving towards him. They are moving closer; their shapes are familiar. It is Goss and Hind.

'Goss!' he calls. 'Hind, hey, over here! I can see a gap.' But his voice is hoarse, inaudible above the noise of the fire.

They have not heard him even though they are close, and they do not stop. They are running past him, Goss in front, Hind following, heading downwards into danger. As the fire chases after them, Barco hears their screams as they run into the blaze and all he can make out are their glowing silhouettes.

Barco stands up and continues, with difficulty, upwards. The boggy ground has made way for the stream. Here the water is cool on his feet and he splashes his face and head, relieved to cool down. Then he scoops up handfuls of mud from the bed of the stream and he smears it over his face and arms and neck — he hopes this will protect him from the effects of the scorching flames. But he must move quickly as the water at his feet is becoming warm.

Now he is almost overcome with the heat but he continues towards the gap at the upper edge. He coughs, takes one huge in-breath, and runs forward, leaping between the fallen trunks. The noise of the trees catching behind him and the crashing branches continues — the forest is alive, dancing and leaping from the ground, exploding, shattering, bursting into flame.

33

Worro is restless; he is sniffing at the air, barking, nudging at the door. He goes over to Dorca, pulls at her clothes, licks her chin, and then he is back at the door. Carew has already gone to the Gathering Hall to meet with the other elders. He has promised to return within the hour, and he has left Worro behind with Dorca.

'Worro, what is it?' Dorca asks. Worro is nudging at her hand and he won't leave her alone. He goes to the door and comes back to her, over and over.

'All right, I want to see what's going on too. You'll have to help me.'

As if Worro understands what she is saying he tries to help her over to the doorway. He gently pulls Dorca along, nudging her with his body as she pulls herself along until she reaches the door. As soon as she reaches up to open it Worro leaps outside.

As with all the Peakerfolk, Dorca is familiar with the ways of the forest from the distance of over-dwellers, and now she realizes that there is something different about the forest as soon as the door is open. The mists are thicker than usual and now the odour of smoke, a foul vapour, is creeping towards lower reaches of the Mountain.

Worro is already outside pulling at the leather rope of the sled and soon he pulls it close to Dorca. With great effort she pulls herself up and onto the seat. Before long they are slipping along the Mountain path towards the Gathering Hall, or so Dorca thinks. Unexpectedly, Worro turns downward onto the Forest path pulling the sled at great speed.

'Worro,' Dorca shouts. 'Turn back!'

Dorca pulls sharply at the reins. She thought that Worro was heading to the Gathering Hall.

But Worro has pulled the sled adrift, away from the path and towards the forest. The Wolfdog slows reluctantly on hearing her command, but will not turn back. He has a mind of his own and now Dorca is coughing and waving away the smoke with her gloved hand.

'Worro, stop!' Dorca calls, choking on the smoke.

Worro relents and the sled comes to a halt not far from the edge of the forest. Dorca's eyes are stinging, and she can hardly see. Now and again there are gaps in the smoke and she can see the muddy ground where the ice has melted with the heat of the fire. Worro is pulling at something on the ground, nudging at it, shaking and dragging a large bag of cloth.

'Worro, what are you doing?' Dorca shouts. 'Leave it alone. Back now. Back.'

But he carries on and then he is barking and barking.

'What is it Worro?' Dorca says, now curious. She sees that the bundle is moving and she fears it is an injured bear or some strange creature that has escaped the fire in the forest.

'Worro, leave it alone,' she pleads.

She pulls as hard as she can at the rein and this time Worro turns his head towards her and growls. The blackened thing is turning over. It is alive. A hand is rising into the air, and Dorca sees that there is someone beneath the blackened clothes. Whoever it is, is still alive. Worro is yapping and yelping and licking at the mud covered face, and soon he has cleaned it enough for her to see the visage.

'Barco?' Dorca says, 'is that you? Is that really you?'

Barco sits up, slowly, he rubs the dirt from his eyes. He embraces Worro who continues to nuzzle and lick him.

'Good to see you, Worro,' Barco says, laughing. 'And you too, Dorca.'

'Barco?' Dorca is hardly able to speak. 'Are you injured?'

'No, I'm all right. It's just mud,' Barco reassures her. 'But we don't have much time. I have seen the Wolfman. I must go to the caves.'

'Are you mad?' Dorca exclaims. 'Let's get you home. The fire's getting worse. You might be injured.'

Barco is getting to his feet but he drops to the ground, suddenly fatigued. 'But first...'

'Worro,' Dorca's voice demands. 'Bring him here, come on boy, here.'

Worro obeys Dorca this time. Barco is half dragged by the Wolfdog towards the sled. Dorca reaches down and with the help of Worro pulls him onto the sled. She untangles the rein that has caught around Worro's leg and once he is in front of the sled she shouts — 'Go!'

34

All is darkness. Maysun is feeling her way along the slippery walls, her feet pressing from heel to toe, tentatively rolling out each step on a floor that is hard and unwelcoming. It is so hot, stifling, as if there is a thick blanket thrown over her, pressing against her face, engulfing her. She fears she will not be able to carry on for long. She is desperately tired, and she longs to rest; even the rush of fear does not give her extra strength. The walls and the ground beneath her feet are her only guides, but even the walls slip beneath her fingers until there is nothing to hold onto, nothing to clutch, no fissures in the rock, no loosening sand; leaving a void of the unknown. Not even the mud of the swamplands is as frictionless as this, and here, even the dark is uncertain.

She turns, thinking she will try to retrace her steps. All she knows is that she must escape from this place, go back to the mountain where the air is cold, but the path is firm underfoot. She wonders if the strange old man has shown her the route to her own death.

The sounds of rumbling and cracking are sending fear into her heart.

She has turned and turned again, and now she reaches out into the void. Nowhere is there light; not forward, behind, above or below. Engulfed in blackness, she cries out, desperate, sinking onto the floor. She lies there and waits: for sleep, for help, for death.

She remains there for what seems like an eternity, drifting in and out of half-consciousness, half-panic, her mind gliding around. At one time she believes she is floating, but she knows that she cannot be as underneath her is the hard floor of the mountain. She thinks she feels water rising, playing around her, beckoning for her to dip beneath the surface. And before she can do anything she is sinking and somehow she knows she must push her arms forward and up, pulling them down to her sides and repeating over and over. Is she swimming or is she dreaming?

It is no longer dark in her dreamworld and she is at the bottom of a deep pool. Something is moving towards her — long and curving, dipping, diving, circling around her. For a moment, she is afraid and then she recognises the creature — the rope-like body, the long neck and the tiny fins that float around, flapping, opening, swishing one way and then the other. She can see the nub of the nose, the retracted lower jaw, the cowl of an eye coming closer until it is staring at her, and she sees her own reflection in its iris. It is the Deathfish that Pa keeps in the tank. As if she is meeting an old friend, she smiles and the Deathfish opens its mouth. A bubble emerges and floats towards her.

She reaches out to catch it as it rises, and rises, until it touches the surface and disappears. Maysun reaches the surface and she is gasping for breath. She awakes fully and understands that she is on the floor of the dark tunnel, the water was not real. Suddenly she sees a faint light ahead of her, a light that was not there before. She can see that the passageway opens out into a chamber. She follows it and comes to an opening, like a bright glade. She gasps. It is like the sunrise when it comes over the hills, or the moment when the light strikes across the water of the lake, bright and piercing. But this opening is wide. She is in a large cavern lined with crystals along each side, and when she looks up, she sees that the roof is encrusted with more gems than she has seen stars in the night sky. There are gaps in the roof of the cavern where the sunlight enters and illuminates the crystals and a pool of still, dark water is at its centre.

The Peakerfolk must use this place to keep their water she thinks, and then she looks around, fearful that she is being watched. But she is alone as far as she can see.

As she approaches the pool, it comes alive with movement and hundreds of bubbles. She looks in and then she sees them. The Wingfish. At least, they look like Wingfish, but they are different, they do not have wings, but they are so alike that they must be related.

They are crowding along the side now, coming towards her, their bodies writhing and churning, causing ripples and waves that patter against the edges. Without thinking, she moves her hand swiftly one way and then the other. And then she is calling, 'Kiri Quar Kiri.' At once, the fish swell, gathering and moving towards her along the surface, mouthing, but not rising. It is as if they are trying to lift themselves, pushing over each other, mounting, prising with their mouths, but then all at once, together, they fall, descending into the depths.

Maysun is dismayed. She has never seen water creatures like these before. Even the Deathfish have cloak-like fins that appear to be wings even if they cannot fly. But these poor creatures know how to fly, she sees it in their movements, in their response to her call. But instead of wings they have stumps; tender looking growths, purple-bruised lumps.

And then she knows. These are Wingfish. These are the progeny of the Wingfish that were brought up to the mountain long ago. But they have had their wings removed. Such cruelty! These are the Wingfish she must save, the ones she heard about from the GrandOmma. She must reunite them with their kin.

From behind her, from the direction from which she

came, she hears the baying of a Wolfdog. They must have followed her here. She trembles. The sound of barking is becoming louder, it is coming closer. The noise is louder, exacerbated as it echoes along the passageways. She hears voices too, strange utterances, harsh sounding words. She looks at the eyeglass in her hand, and she holds it up for a second — it has become a swirl of red, flowing around like a pool of blood.

35

'We must build a barrier and wait,' Carew says to the crowd in the Gathering Hall. Carew describes how a team of people could form a high snow-barrier at the edge of the forest. He believes that the only way to stop the forest fire is to build a barrier, one that would slow the flames and quench the fire.

Jagg pushes forward. Pointing at Carew he says: 'You're crazy, no one's listening to you.'

The crowd is jostling and many of them are looking to Jagg to know what to do.

'Let's go before the smoke chokes us to death,' Jagg says. 'We need to get to the deep caves. To shut ourselves away. At least we have water there and food.' He laughs. 'Smoked Wingfish anyone?' The crowd cheer.

They all turn and begin to leave the hall. Carew shrugs his shoulders and follows them outside. What else can he do? He has obviously lost his role as "Leader" but in a way he is relieved as he no longer has any answers. Already the smoke has ascended the mountain, billowing above the Marginlands. Wisps are floating into the Gathering Hall — the place that has been a refuge for all these years. If the fire continues with its current progress it will devour the Gathering Hall and all in its way — every shack and shed and lean-to that form the clusters of buildings nearby, the few crops and plants that are left will be smoked out, burned to the ground. It will be the end of the Peakerfolk.

Perhaps Jagg, for once, is right — there is only one place to go and that is into the Mountain. But Carew does not trust the Mountain, he never has. He thinks of Dorca, his only daughter, waiting for him at home to arrive with news, with a plan, but there is nothing he can say. He must hurry back to her. All they can do now is to go to the caves with the lakes and stay there until the fire has passed. He has never liked the darkness there, the still air that festers within the rocks of the Mountain. Carew shudders at the thought.

Carew walks briskly towards his home cave. He likes to be outside, to breathe the chilled air of the mountain, to feel the crisp brightness of the sun on his face, and to hear the trickling of the snowmelt streams. These are the things that make him feel alive. The taint of smoke has taken that away. Now, as he reaches the cave he sees that it is in darkness. Dorca hasn't even lit the tallow candle — at least it would have given her a little warmth, and there is no glow coming from below the door of the cave entrance. He calls her name, but there is no reply, the cave is empty. The sled is gone, as are Dorca and Worro.

He follows the path back to the underground caves. It is crowded with Peakerfolk, jostling to enter the caves. Some have already gone inside, others are milling around, pushing their belongings into backpacks, explaining to their children what is happening, pointing to the mountain and back to the rising smoke of the forest. Carew begins to panic. What has happened to Dorca? He asks people if they know where she is but everyone is intent on trying to get into the caves, and no one has seen her. As the crowd thins, Carew notices the sled, their family sled, and there is Dorca wrapped up, smiling at him. Worro barks in greeting.

'Dorca,' Carew says, relieved. 'How did you get here? And why are you here? You know how dangerous it is to come out alone.'

'It was Worro,' she says. 'We found Barco and then we came here, and now he's gone into the cave.' She is speaking quickly trying to explain everything at once.

'Barco? Barco is back?' Carew is confused but his eyes brighten at the glimmer of hope.

'Yes,' Dorca continues. 'He's gone inside,' Dorca says, and looks worried, 'he said something about the Wolfman.'

'Wolfman? What Wolfman? Is he injured?'

'Hardly,' Dorca says. 'He's worried about a girl and the Wingfish.'

'What are you talking about?' Carew is looking confused.

'And now Jagg has gone in too.'

Most of the Peakerfolk have entered the cave system and they can be heard talking and jostling as they make their way through the antechamber, and then the sounds lessen, and finally they fade until Dorca and Carew can only hear a dull rumble.

'Now they will be arriving at the split in the passageway,' says Carew. He can remember going into the caves with his grandfather and learning how the double passageways had been formed to fool their enemies, should ever the Peakerfolk need to escape.

'Only a few know the way,' Carew murmurs, 'to the Wingfish caves.'

The smoke outside is thickening and through the billowing gaps Carew sees the peak of the Mountain, stark against the sky. It becomes blurred as a black plume of smoke ascends from the forest, glittering with orange sparks.

It is then that Carew understands that he and Dorca can no longer remain in the world of the Peakerfolk.

36

Maysun knows she must find a way out. But first she must gather the Wingfish. She looks around the cave to see if there is something she might use to carry them in. She sees a trough in a dark corner. It is made from a gouged out tree trunk and fixed onto the runners of a sled. It looks old and worn and has probably been abandoned, perhaps because of the cracks in the body.

The Wingfish are unable to fly so she cannot call them or gather them with the spell of her voice. She must find another way to persuade them to come to her, to trust her. From her pockets she takes the pouch; the one she has stuffed with leaves from the stream. They are not Gringrows but they will have to suffice; and there are at least a few Gringrow fronds from her pocket that she can give to them, to tempt them. She holds the pouch below the waterline and slowly, the Wingfish swim towards her, made curious by the wavering leaves, but then they swim away to the far side. Why should they trust her? It could be a trap. Have they not been tricked before?

'Kir Quar Kiri,' she calls, softly over and over.

There is a single ripple that runs across the surface of the lake. The Wingfish know the words, the sound, the call. More ripples run and lap one over the other. The movement gathers speed, the Wingfish are circling the pool and then breaking into smaller circles that spiral towards Maysun. When they reach the near edge she scoops them out of the water and she lays them on the leaves, wrapping them up in the foliage and then placing them into the trough. She scoops out as much water as she can with her hands to fill the shallow trough. They hardly move; they are stilled by the ululation of her voice. Finally, she lowers her voice and whispers to them. The lives of the Wingfish will be suspended for only as long as it takes to return them to the lake in the valley.

37

Barco is struggling to move through the passageways. Not only are his feet sore and blistered from his trek through the burning Ruba forest but he is finding it hard to breathe. The smoke from the forest is beginning to find its way into the cave system. He can hear Worro barking. He knows that the Wolfdog is waiting patiently outside with Dorca, and that he is anxious not to lose sight of his master, Barco, again. The Wolfman had been very clear, he had urged him to go to the caves, and that he must hurry to the Wingfish pool, but as yet, he does not know why. Barco can hardly see where he is going until he gets to the point when the passage opens out into the lit crystal chamber. When he arrives by the large lake the girl is crouched by the edge of the pool.

In the glimmering light of the cave, Barco can just make out the girl's face. She has the features of a Watterishi. He looks around to see if there is anyone else inside the cave, but she is alone. As he approaches he realises why the Wolfman has sent him here. The girl is the same one he left in the tree house at the lower edges of the Ruba Forest. He knows it must be so when he sees his jacket on her. It is her: Maysun.

The girl backs further into the corner and turns her face away from Barco as he approaches. Barco looks at the water in the lake expecting to see the Wingfish but it is empty. Then he sees that the sled with the old water trough attached to it is behind the girl and he realises what she has done. She has come to rescue the remaining Wingfish.

'It's all right, I won't hurt you,' Barco says. 'I want to help, I wanted to help you before, and I... I was going to go back for you.' She is looking over his shoulder now as if she is terrified.

A shout is coming from the passageway. It is a man's voice, one that Barco knows only too well. It is Jagg and he is followed by a crowd, their voices resounding, echoing through the passageways, rebounding from every wall. Barco knows that there is a secret exit from the Wingfish cavern but it is many years since he has been there, and he hopes it is not blocked. The noise of the throng increases, becoming louder and louder as they approach the Wingfish cavern.

Barco backs away putting his finger to his lips to indicate to the girl that they should remain quiet. He beckons to Maysun and points to a place in the rock where the shadows are creased. The shouting from the passageway increases. Barco beckons to Maysun again as he walks towards the rock and disappears behind it for a moment, and then he re-appears encouraging her to follow. She does not move at first but appears to be frozen in fear.

'Omma?' Barco says. He has remembered the word that the girl repeated in the treehouse.

The girl looks at him, startled. She looks confused. Barco edges back towards the opening in the rock. He beckons to her, more urgently now. Maysun is holding tightly onto the strap that is attached to the trough and when she pulls it towards her, it rumbles over the cavern floor.

Maysun follows Barco and they disappear into the dark shadow of the rock just as Jagg and his posse enter the Wingfish cavern.

38

Soon the pinch of the cold night air nips at their faces and Maysun can see a pocket of stars in the sky ahead of them where the tunnel opens out. First they enter an ante-chamber, and then they are outside on the Mountain. Below them, is a rolling sea of grey; clouds of smoke that have smothered the trees like feathery pillows.

Barco helps Maysun to lift the trough-sled out onto the Mountain track and they stand there for a moment, gazing at the scene below. Something or someone is approaching from around the ridge — an undulating shadow is sliding around the rock and along the ice towards them. A sled. It slows and come to a halt; Worro barks and leaps up, becoming tangled in the reins that are held by Dorca. Carew sits next to her on the sled and there are two empty seats behind them, back to back.

'Stop it Worro!' Dorca calls. She is relieved that they have found Barco again, and smiles at the girl. 'Come on,' she says, 'there's no time to lose.'

But Maysun is backing away. She is terrified at the sight of the Wolfdog.

'It's all right, it's Worro,' Barco says.

It is only then that Maysun realises that this is the large Wolfdog that chased the others away during the attack on the Wingfish at the edge of the Ruba Forest.

'We will help you,' continues Barco. 'We are setting off for your land. There is nothing more here for us.'

She ties the trough-sled with its precious contents of Wingfish to the back of Dorca's sled. Maysun is hesitant as she looks down at the forest, now almost concealed by smoke. She knows that she has no other choice — she must return home with the Wingfish. She will take her precious cargo to join their kin in the Gringrow lake. The storm is returning and they hear a rumble of thunder. Maysun checks that the Wingfish are cool and wrapped in the leaves and she is pleased that the rain is beginning to fall.

Worro stretches and arches his back as if to test the weight of the sled. Maysun climbs on board with Barco, they pull the bear skin over them. Dorca flicks the reins, and shouts for Worro to move forward.

The sled begins to move down the icy track. Everything creaks as they set off, as the rotten sides of the old water trough groan. At first they wobble from side to side on the ice with the addition of the new passengers and the trough sled, but then, as they gather speed, they slip away clean and fast towards the Marginlands and the upper edge of the Ruba forest.

The storm increases; the rain turns, water drops become stones of ice, the sky flickers with lightning and followed by a roar of thunder the rocks split and tumble down the mountain alongside the sled as it travels towards the ever increasing smoke. Dorca snaps at the reins until Worro pelts as fast as fear. They enter the cut-through track that has hardly been marked by the fire since the wind has quickly shifted sending the fire westwards, leaving a swathe of steaming, smouldering Ruba in its wake.

A plume rises behind them as ash falls from the sky and a single cry can be heard as they disappear into the forest towards the valleys of the Watterishi.

'Kiri Quar Kiri!'

Mother's Milk Books
is an independent press, founded and managed by
at-home mother, Dr Teika Bellamy.

The aim of the press is to celebrate femininity
and empathy through images and words,
with a view to normalizing breastfeeding.
The annual Mother's Milk Books Writing Prize, which
welcomes poetry and prose from both adults and children,
runs from September to mid-January.
Mother's Milk Books also produces and sells art
and poetry prints, as well as greetings cards.
For more information about the press, and to make purchases
from the online store,
please visit: www.mothersmilkbooks.com